JACKIE BLUE
A JUSTICE SECURITY NOVEL
By
T. M. Bilderback

Author's note: While I try to write each of the Justice Security novels as a stand-alone story, sometimes it isn't possible. Parts of previous novels play into others. While Jackie Blue can be enjoyed by itself, the story is enhanced if you've read the first book in the series, Mama Told Me Not To Come. If you have read Mama, you'll enjoy the continuity. If you haven't, you'll enjoy this story on its own merits. Mostly, I thank you for choosing to read the story.

- T. M. Bilderback

Chapter 1

Vincent Lambosa enjoyed his job.

Vincent was an enforcer for the Giambini mob in the city. He had started when he was sixteen as a numbers runner for a local bookie. Occasionally, the bookie would dispatch Vincent and another guy to visit welshers to "discuss payment options" with them. Vincent threw himself into his work quite vigorously, which resulted in a near one hundred percent "collection" record. This perfect record caught the attention of people higher up in the organization. These people began keeping an eye on Vincent.

When Vincent was eighteen, he was invited to meet with Leo Lesko. Lesko was in charge of a string of bookies in the organization, which made him Vincent's boss's boss.

Vincent met with Leo in a booth at McFeely's Bar on Third Street. McFeely's, referred to as "McFeelme's" on the street, was known for serving hard drinks to harder customers, and had been in the same location for fifteen years at the time of the meeting. Third Street had become seedy, and was just beginning to earn its nickname of "Hooker Hollow".

"Vincent," said Lesko, who gestured for him to sit down. "Thanks for coming."

Vincent nodded his acknowledgement, then sat across from Lesko.

"I'll get straight to the point, Vincent. We think your boss is skimming a little extra something off the top."

"I don't know nothin' about that, Mr. Lesko."

Lesko nodded. "We know you don't, Vincent." He drank beer, set it down, and continued. "What we need from you is to kinda keep your eyes open for us. We want you to observe your boss, watch for anything unusual, and let us know what you see. Can you do that for us, Vincent?"

Lesko watched as Vincent rolled the possibilities around inside his head. If he outright refused to do what was asked, his life wouldn't be worth a plug nickel. If he agreed to do what Lesko asked, then didn't follow up...same result.

If he reported false information, and Lesko found out about it, again his life wouldn't be worth a plug nickel. But...if he did as he was asked...he would be trusted, and could advance in the organization.

"Sure, Mr. Lesko," said Vincent. "I can do that. What will I be watching for? And how will I get it to you?"

Lesko told him.

VINCENT SPENT THE NEXT four weeks watching his boss. He discovered that it was difficult to watch without giving himself away, but he watched...and watched.

Finally, he saw what Lesko had told him to watch for...and it disappointed him. He had thought – or maybe *hoped* – that his boss was an honest crook.

He found a pay phone and dialed the number that Lesko had given him. He was surprised when Lesko himself answered.

"Lesko."

"Mr. Lesko, this is Vincent Lambosa."

"Vincent!" Vincent could hear the smile in Lesko's voice. "It's good to hear from you...or maybe, not so good."

"Mr. Lesko, I don't know if it's good or not. I been watching, like you said to. I saw it happen – what you told me to watch for. I saw him."

Lesko was silent for a moment. "Thank you, Vincent. I want to compliment you on your observational skills. Not everyone would have seen what I mentioned to you. I'll be in touch."

"Thank you, Mr. Lesko."

That was the first time that Vincent had used his God-given observational talents. Of course, he was no fool – he knew that his observations had just cost his boss his life. He justified it to himself two ways: One, his boss should not have been skimming profits. Two, *better him than me.*

NOW, FIFTEEN YEARS later, Vincent had advanced considerably in the organization. As a result of his excellent skills in the area of "collections", he was now in charge of three strings of bookies. And he was in charge of the "protection service" for the south side of the city.

He still performed many of his own collections, which were primarily for his "protection service". His observational skills had proven to serve him well in conducting that particular business. He would spend a couple of months observing a prospective protection client so that he could accurately judge its business traffic. Then, he would quote an accurate and, to him, affordable "insurance" rate for the client. The unfortunate businesses that refused his "insurance" often suddenly caught fire in the middle of the night and burned to the ground, despite any fire suppression devices that might be present.

A few weeks ago, Vincent had been observing business at a small convenience store, *Kwikstuff,* which was located five blocks down and three blocks over from the Hollow. He had been watching the Pakistani proprietor ring up various sodas, cigarettes, and lottery tickets, when Vincent happened to see the oddest thing.

A slim, pretty blonde, probably in her early – or maybe middle – thirties came into the store. She stood in front of the plexiglass cabinet that housed the store's supply of scratch-off lottery tickets. She reached out and ran her fingers lightly along the front of the cabinet in a back-and-forth motion, until she stopped her hand in front of one of the plexiglass cubicles and closed her eyes. When she opened her eyes, she went to the checkout and purchased one scratch-off ticket from the cubicle that had captured her attention. She then sat down at one of the dining tables in the front of the store, and scratched off her ticket. When she had finished, she stood, and returned to the checkout counter.

The Pakistani smiled at the woman. "Another winner, Jackie?"

The woman smiled and nodded.

The Pakistani ran her ticket through the store's lottery scanner. "Wow! Two hundred dollars this time!" He shook his head as he paid her the money. "Do you *ever* lose, Jackie?"

The woman smiled and shrugged, tucked her money into her jeans, and left the store.

Vincent had picked up a tin of breath mints and taken them to the cash register. He smiled at the Pakistani with a smile that didn't reach his eyes. "She wins a lot, I take it."

The Pakistani shook his head. "I have never seen anything like it! She *never* loses!"

"Maybe I should ask her for a date. Do you know her name?"

The Pakistani nodded. "Her name is Jacqueline Belew, but I don't think she dates much. I've never seen her with a guy."

Vincent nodded, as if making a decision. "Interesting. A challenge. Much like running a business. Let me talk to you about something..." Vincent then explained the benefits of having his "company's protection". After some vigorous, intense negotiations in the back room, which caused Vincent's knuckles to swell a bit, he was able to count the humbled and bruised Pakistani as one of his customers.

VINCENT AGAIN OBSERVED the Belew woman the following week, at a different retail establishment. She entered, and again ran her hand along the market's plexiglass ticket cabinet. She made her selection, purchased it, and scratched it off. And again, she took the ticket to the cashier, collected her three hundred dollar winnings, and left the store. Vincent, having concluded his business in the store, chose to follow her.

Vincent watched from behind the tinted windshield of his car as she walked. If she got too far ahead of him, he would drive down the street until he was ahead of her, the watch her approach in his rearview mirror.

Jacqueline hailed a taxi and climbed in. Vincent waited until it passed, then pulled into traffic to follow. The taxi got onto the freeway. Vincent stayed three car lengths behind. After fifteen minutes, the taxi took an exit. She was going to the race track!

Now that Vincent knew where Jacqueline was going, he relaxed. He passed the taxi at his first opportunity, and arrived at the track first. A few minutes later, his face partially obscured by a racing paper, Vincent observed Jacqueline going through the entrance to the track. After she passed, he followed her.

Jacqueline got a racing form. Vincent watched as she ran her finger down the sheet. Her finger stopped. She went to the betting window, placed a bet, and tucked the receipt into her purse. As she walked out to watch the race, Vincent followed. The race was about to start.

He watched as the gates opened and the horses began their race. Jacqueline didn't really watch the race – she kept glancing at her wristwatch, as if she were late for something. The race ended, and the winner was a 35-to-1 long shot named, "Joe's Folly". Vincent watched as Jacqueline returned to the betting window and retrieved her betting receipt from her purse. After showing identification, the ticket agent handed her a large wad of one hundred dollar bills. She apparently had wagered the three hundred dollars she had won from the scratch-off ticket on the 35-to-1 long shot. She had pocketed over ten thousand dollars!

Vincent began to get an idea...if what he believed was actually happening, he may have found a gold mine for the organization!

JACQUELINE LEFT THE track, oblivious to the man following her. She hailed a taxi, and climbed in to head for home. If she hurried, she could meet the bus at the house and could help the kids inside. She told the driver her address, and told him that a large tip would be involved if he got her there quickly.

Jacqueline had a gift. She was able to pick the winner from any game of chance. *Any* game of chance, be it a lottery ticket, horse race, sports game, sweepstakes...once, even a turkey shoot. She always knew the outcome, and in games that she participated in, she was always the winner.

Growing up, she soon realized that not everyone could do what she did. Her friends eventually stopped playing even board games with her, because she always won...not by cheating, but by *knowing* what moves to make to give herself the advantage. Her best friend from high school, Dawn Price, once said to her, "Jackie, what's a game, if you never lose? It stops being a game if you win all the time!" Jacqueline took that remark to heart. She used her gift, but never for much...and only to help the kids.

Today's win at the track had been a tremendous windfall. Once a month, Jacqueline would take her scratch off winnings to the race track to try to multiply her winnings, but long shots like Joe's Folly didn't happen to her often. When they did, it was usually just in time to buy an unusual item that one of the kids needed. Like today's win – it would cover the cost of repairing Jennie Lou's wheelchair, and buy some clothes for the boys – they grew so fast! – and a few groceries, and maybe leave a little left over to take the kids out for McDonalds'...or maybe pizza.

Jacqueline Belew was a foster mom to five special needs kids. The state paid a pittance to support them and her group home, but it wasn't enough to keep them healthy, fed, clothed, and safe. If it wasn't for her gift, she didn't know what she'd do.

VINCENT WAS FOLLOWING the taxi. His mind was working as he drove, trying to work out the details...and, as always, his observational skills were functioning at the subconscious level. He observed the various residential street names, and remembered each one. When he saw the taxi stop at a large, two-story, comfortable-looking frame house on Peach Street, he observed the house number, without even thinking about it, as he drove past and turned right at the next street.

He decided that he needed to observe Jacqueline Belew a little longer. He needed an edge.

VINCENT OBSERVED HIS edge forty-five minutes later.

Earlier, when he had turned right at the next street, he turned right again. He then parked on this street – Cherry Street – and got out of his car. He crossed the back yard of a house facing Cherry Street, into the back yard of a house facing Peach Street. He knocked on the back door of the house.

A few seconds later, a woman opened the door. Vincent convinced her to allow him access to her home by demonstrating his forty-five semiautomatic's gleeful stainless steel shine in the bright sunlight. Once inside, he overcame the woman's strenuous objections by demonstrating the semiautomatic's prowess at delivering a small piece of metal into her head. He then provided the woman a singular opportunity to examine the processes involved in mimicking a frozen bag of vegetables from the interior of her chest-type freezer.

Taking the lack of objection from the woman as an invitation to make himself at home, Vincent then toured the house. In the master bedroom, he discovered a pair of binoculars. No objection to his use of them came from inside the freezer, so Vincent pleasantly took the visual aids into the living room, and focused them on the house belonging to Jacqueline Belew.

Jacqueline had time to make a pitcher of lemonade before the special school bus arrived. It stopped in front of the house, with its doors perfectly even with the sidewalk. The driver, Mike Woods, cheerfully honked the bus's horn with a "shave and a haircut" tune, which always made Jacqueline smile.

As she headed outside, she picked up a storage container that held cookies that she had baked with the kids the previous evening. When she got to the curb, Mike the bus driver had already opened the doors and helped two of the kids out. Both children were boys, and both wore leg braces. They turned to the bus and each held out a hand. A girl, also wearing leg braces, along with metal crutches attached to her wrists and held tightly in her hands, was standing in the bus's doorway. She looked down at the two boys, smiled, and gave one of her hands to each of them. They held tight to her as she worked her way down the steps.

"Thank you, gentlemen," said the girl, with a mock English accent. She worked herself away from the door of the bus, then turned back.

Jacqueline, meanwhile, had stopped beside Mike and was watching this exchange. Jacqueline smiled.

"I guess I've taught them well, Mike. They're a real family now," she said quietly to the big bus driver.

"They sure look out for each other, Miss Jackie," said Mike. Then, under his breath, he said to her, "Phillip is *really* protective of her today. He got really antsy while I was helping her onto the bus at school."

Jacqueline looked concerned, and said under her breath, "Did he give you any trouble?"

Mike shook his head. "No, but he really started rocking. Jennie Lou calmed him down a little, but he was still agitated."

The young man who was being discussed, Phillip Wheeler, stepped off of the bus, carrying a folded wheelchair. He quickly assembled it, then climbed back onto the bus. A few minutes later, he came down the steps of the bus with a girl in his arms. He gently placed her in her wheelchair, snapped the armrests into place, and put the girl's hand onto a joystick controller. When he had finished, he stood straight...but rocked back and forth in place, looking at nothing.

Autism sucks, thought Jackie.

Phillip had been with Jackie for seven years. She had no idea what his back history was – a juvenile court judge had sealed the files permanently.

As she watched Jennie Lou Gwin struggle with the joystick, Jackie also cursed the automobile accident that had placed Jennie Lou into the wheelchair five years ago. Jennie Lou was almost a quadriplegic, but she did have *some* use of her right hand, and she could lift her head. The accident had killed her parents and her brother. She had been with Jackie for three years.

Phillip had attached himself to Jennie Lou from the beginning. Jennie accepted Phillip's care for her, and often confided in him. Perhaps in a subconscious way, Jennie recognized that Phillip needed her as much as she needed him, and Jackie feared how far into himself Phillip would have retreated if it hadn't been for Jennie Lou.

Jennie Lou was sixteen. Phillip was seventeen. Phillip was two inches over six feet, and was very muscular. He could hurt someone without meaning to, but Jennie Lou kept him calm.

Mostly.

The two boys with the leg braces were Nicky Watson and Tommy Larkin. Nicky had had a bout with polio, and had left his legs almost useless. He had never received the polio vaccine...his mother had been a crack whore, and hadn't bothered with what she considered unnecessary things, like food, clothing, or medical care for her son. She had overdosed and died while entertaining a client in her filthy bedroom. Her client noticed that she had stopped breathing, but finished his business anyway. When he was done, he got dressed, and left. Nicky was alone for two days before he was discovered and taken to Children's Services. He was Jackie's first foster child, and had been with her for eight years. He claimed that he didn't remember his real mom.

Tommy had been born into a well-off upper middle class family. His father had been a successful banking executive...up until the time that the bottom fell out of the real estate market. The successful banking executive suddenly became a jobless individual facing possible indictment for loan fraud. The man came home with a smile on his face, stabbed his loving wife twelve times with the butcher knife from the kitchen, and had left his son for dead with several stab wounds...one of which had been low on his spinal cord, and had nearly severed it. Tommy's father then went out to the storage shed beside the inground swimming pool, took out the push mower, started the engine, turned it on its side, and shoved both arms into the whirling blades almost up to the elbows. He bled to death in his own back yard, while laughing at the sky. Doctors were able to reconstruct and reconnect much of Tommy's nerves, but he still didn't have full use of his legs...hence the leg braces. Tommy was the newest addition to the group home – he had been there for a year. He still had nightmares of his father's lunatic grin as he stabbed his only child repeatedly.

Nicky was thirteen, and Tommy was twelve.

The young girl with the braces and canes was Cynthia Rudisill. Cynthia had cerebral palsy. It was a mild case, but crippling nonetheless. Cynthia's mother had decided that CP was more than she could bear in today's society, so she had simply taken the child to Children's Services and left her, much as she would have taken a stray dog to the pound. The woman's conscience did not bother her one bit about what she had done...as far as she was concerned, she had simply disposed of a hassle. Cynthia had been with Jackie for six years. Cynthia's mother had spent two years in state prison for child abandonment, and had her parental rights terminated. She didn't much care, and moved across the country when she was released from state custody. Cynthia's father was not listed on her birth certificate, and none of her mother's family was interested in taking on a cerebral palsy child into their home. Cynthia was twelve.

These special needs children had all came to Jacqueline and her group home. Jackie's house rules were simple: Love each other. Look out for each other. Accept each other as siblings, and know that Jackie loves them all unflinchingly and unconditionally. In all ways but biological, Jacqueline *was* the mother of these kids...and would do anything for them.

Her nickname, Jackie Blue, had come from Phillip. He had not been very vocal when she first met him. After repeatedly telling him her name, Jackie had asked him to repeat it.

"Jackie *Blue!*" he had shouted. The name had stuck, and each kid had adopted it.

Jackie was amused, and accepted it with good grace. It was kind of appealing to her.

"Kids!" called Jackie. "Hey, *kids!*" They all turned to look at her, the lone exception being Phillip. He continued to stare at nothing, but she knew he heard her.

"Should we offer Mr. Mike something?" she said as she shook the plastic cookie container.

Realization dawned on each of the children's faces. Shouts of "Cookies!" and "Mr. Mike, we made cookies!" and "Please try one, Mr. Mike!" echoed each other. All of the children were smiling, even Phillip, and they all gathered around the big bus driver.

Laughing, Mike said, "Okay, ya big buncha rats! Give a guy some room, will ya?" Kids were laughing and smiling as the big man took a cookie from the container that Jacqueline held. He took a bite, and a look of pleasure crossed his face. "Peanut butter! My favorite kind!"

The kids all took turns saying, "I'm glad!" or "Peanut butter was *my* idea!" Phillip actually stopped rocking long enough to say, "Mike likes peanut butter!"

Jacqueline turned to the bus driver. "Mr. Mike, thank you for bringing my kids home safe once more." She kissed him on the cheek.

Mike Woods blushed deeply and looked at the ground. "Just doin' my job, Miss Jackie," he said, sheepishly.

Suddenly, all the gathered kids gave Mike a hug. Even Phillip put an arm around the bus driver and patted him on the back.

Jaqueline, smiling, said, "Okay, kids, there's lemonade inside to go with the cookies and homework. Let's go!" She clapped her hands. The children all turned toward the house, with Phillip pushing Jennie Lou's wheelchair. They all waved to Mike and shouted things like "Bye!" and "See you in the morning!" The driver climbed back into his bus as the family went inside the house.

"Closer than most *related* families," said Mike to himself, as he climbed into his bus and watched the family go inside the house.

VINCENT LOWERED HIS complimentary binoculars. *A house full of crips and retards,* he thought.

This was going to be easier than he thought.

THAT NIGHT, JACKIE was tucking all of the children into bed. Phillip, as the oldest, had his own room. Jackie tucked Jennie Lou in and kissed her, did the same for Cynthia, and told them that she loved them. She then did the same for Nicky and Tommy.

Jackie went to Phillip's room. Phillip was sitting on his bed, in his pajamas, facing his window. He was rocking back and forth. Jackie was concerned, because Phillip only rocked when he was worried.

"Phillip, what's wrong?" she asked him. She didn't expect an answer, because he had difficulty vocalizing when he was upset. He simply rocked a bit faster.

Jackie put her hand on his shoulder and looked at his face. His eyes were focused on the window. She turned to look outside.

There were police cars and an ambulance at Mrs. Morgan's across the street. Neighbors were gathered on the sidewalk, behind "crime scene do not cross" yellow tape. Something bad must have happened.

"Phillip," Jackie said, "you shouldn't worry about Mrs. Morgan. I'm sorry that something seems to have happened at her house, but it's nothing for you to worry about. You're safe here at home."

She gently eased the boy back into the bed and covered him up. She kissed him on the forehead. Phillip seemed to relax, and he closed his eyes.

"Good night, shining knight," whispered Jackie. The boy smiled slightly, and fell asleep.

THE NEXT MORNING, AFTER the kids had left for school, Jackie walked two blocks over to the bus stop. She caught the bus into town, and got off close to *Kwikstuff,* the Pakistani's convenience store.

Vincent was following her.

Chapter 2

When Jackie walked into the convenience store, the first thing she noticed was the bruised store owner. His left eye was swollen shut, and his right eye was discolored. There were cuts on his cheeks, which also were swollen. His nose had white bandage tape across it, because it was obviously broken. His lips were swollen almost twice their normal size.

"Malik!" said Jackie. "What happened to you?"

"Oh, Jackie," he replied. "There was a man, and he was asking about y..." Malik broke off his sentence as he noticed the man coming through the entrance door. It was Vincent. "What can I get you today, Jackie?"

Jackie was a little confused by the Pakistani's abrupt change of conversation. "Um...give me a minute, will you, Malik?"

"Of course."

Jackie walked over to the plexiglass cabinet and started doing her thing. Vincent, watching, decided to move closer to her to see how she chose her tickets.

She actually touched the cabinet as she ran her fingers along it.

"Wow," said Vincent conversationally. "I sure wish I knew which ones were winners. I could sure use the extra cash right now."

Jackie glanced up at the man, met his eyes, and smiled at him. "Try the Treasure Trove tickets. I've always had good luck with them." She turned toward Malik, and Vincent followed, fully acting his part now.

"Thanks! I think I *will* try one," he said to her.

"Good luck," she said to Vincent. To Malik, she said, "I'd like one Moneybag Madness, please."

Malik was eyeing Vincent as he went to retrieve the ticket for Jacqueline. He brought it back to the register and rang it up.

"Two dollars, please."

Jackie gave Malik two ones.

"Thank you, Jackie," said Malik. "I hope it is good to you."

Jackie smiled at Malik as she said, "No, thank *you*, Malik, for putting up with me." Jackie took her scratch-off ticket and moved to one of the bench-style tables.

Vincent, meanwhile, moved up to the register. "One Treasure Trove, please." He winked at Malik.

Malik felt a chill down his back as he retrieved the ticket and rang it up. "Two dollars, please."

Vincent said, "Sure." Then, he picked up his ticket and walked to the table that Jackie had taken.

Malik, resigned, closed the register drawer and made a note to himself that the register would be off by two dollars.

"Hope you don't mind me sitting down with you," said Vincent with a smile. He sat opposite Jackie. "I thought it would be nice to scratch our tickets together."

Jackie smiled politely, and said nothing. Something about this man made her slightly uncomfortable...it felt as if she had slid her hand under a rug. She continued scratching off the covered blocks on her card until all of them were uncovered.

Vincent scratched off the blocks on his card, and discovered that he had won a hundred dollars. Surprised, he looked up to tell Jackie about it, but she had risen from the table and gone back to the front counter. Vincent quickly followed. He arrived just in time to see Jackie tuck five one hundred dollar bills into her purse.

"Hey!" he said to her. "This ticket won me a hundred bucks! Thank you!"

Jackie slipped out the door of the market. She acknowledged Vincent's thanks with a wave and another polite smile.

Vincent's smile disappeared from his face, as if it had never been there. To Malik he said, "Gimme my hundred bucks, *fast*, asshole!"

Malik gave Vincent a hundred dollar bill, then watched with relief as Vincent ran out the market's door.

Outside the market, Vincent was in time to see Jackie open the door of a taxi. Jogging over to the taxi, he was in time to say to her, "Say...what's your name?"

Jackie was sitting in the taxi with her hand on the door, preparing to close it. She looked up at Vincent.

"Sir, with all due respect," she said to him, "I don't want to give you my name. For some reason, you frighten me. Please release the door."

Vincent, surprised, took a step back from the taxi.

"Thank you, sir," said Jackie. She then closed the door and the taxi sped away.

Vincent watched the taxi as it drove down the block. If Jackie had turned back and seen the look on Vincent's face, she would have been much more frightened.

Vincent, mumbling to himself, said, "Frighten you, huh, puss? You ain't seen *nuthin'* yet!"

TWO DAYS LATER, JACKIE got the children safely loaded onto Mr. Mike's school bus. She stood outside on the sidewalk, dressed in her bathrobe, until the bus was out of sight. She picked up an advertising paper from the front sidewalk, then returned inside to prepare some breakfast for herself and start her day.

Vincent was sitting at the kitchen table. His shiny semiautomatic was sitting on the table in front of him.

Jackie did not scream. She drew in a startled breath and froze when she saw Vincent, then she pulled the top of her robe together. The feeling of reaching under a rug intensified.

"What are you doing here?" she asked.

Vincent gestured to the chair opposite him.

"Sit down. We're gonna talk."

Jackie said, "Get out now, or I'll call the police."

"Reach for the phone and you'll be dead before you touch it," replied Vincent from under lowered brows. "Then, I'll wait here until the crips and retards get home, and I'll kill every one of them, too. You really don't want to fuck with me on this, puss." He gestured to the chair again. "Now, *sit down!*"

The color began draining from Jackie's face as each word was spoken until she was quite pale. As Vincent said to sit down, she almost jumped. Wordlessly, she sat.

Vincent nodded to her, and said, "Thanks. What I wanna know is easy, Jacqueline Belew. How do you pick winners every time? You got some kinda system or something?"

Jackie, wondering to herself how this frightening man had found out about her gift, tried to bluff her way through. "Look, that was a fluke with the hundred dollars. I had no idea..."

"Sure you didn't," interrupted Vincent. "Just like you didn't have any idea about the five hundred bucks that you tucked into your purse...or the three hundred the other day. Or the long shot at the track." He leaned forward and looked into her eyes. As he leaned, he picked up the pistol and jacked a round into the chamber. "Wanna try again?"

Jackie pleaded, "I really don't know what you're talking about, sir. I know that you won..."

Vincent pointed the gun at her face. "You have until I count to three. Then, you die." He paused. "One."

"Sir, I haven't..." A tear was running down her face.

"Two."

"Why are you doing this?" she cried.

The muscles in Vincent's hand began tightening in anticipation of the recoil. Jackie saw this.

"Thr...," Vincent started.

"I have a gift!" shouted Jackie, half rising from the chair. "I can tell the winner of any game of chance!"

"How?" said Vincent. His gun never wavered from her face.

Jackie sat back down and put her face in her hands. "I can see it in my mind," she replied between fingers. "Whenever chance is a part of an event, I can see the outcome."

Vincent studied her for a moment. Then, he nodded as if he'd made a decision, and put the gun down on the table. "Show me," he said to her.

She looked out from behind her hands. "What?"

"Show me," he repeated.

Jackie looked around the kitchen, then at Vincent. "How?"

Vincent shrugged. "Got a deck of cards?"

"Yes, I think the kids do...," she said, eager to please. She started to rise to retrieve them, but Vincent raised his hand.

"Tell me where the cards are. I'll get them," he said forcefully.

Jackie sat back down. "Of course. They're in the top drawer there." She pointed toward the counter.

Vincent could reach the drawer without rising. He kept a hand on his gun as he leaned over, opened the drawer, and took out a deck of cards.

Jackie's mind was telling her to play along for now – there was no safe way out. She hoped that she lived to see the children again.

Vincent, meanwhile, had opened the box containing the cards and began shuffling them.

"Okay, *Jackie*," he said emphatically. "We're going to play a little twenty-one. Blackjack. I'm guessing you know how to play?"

Jackie nodded.

Vincent dealt one card face down to each of them, then one card up. Jackie's card was a four. Vincent's card was a five. Jackie peeked at her hole card. It was a two.

"Hit me," she said.

Vincent dealt another card, face up. A two.

"Again," she said.

Another two.

"Again."

An ace.

"I'll stay," she said quietly. Since an ace could be either one or eleven, she chose eleven. That gave her a twenty one.

Vincent looked at his hole card. An eight. He took one.

A queen.

Busted.

He folded the cards and tossed them to the side of the table. Jackie turned up her hole card to show that she would have won anyway, then put her cards aside.

Vincent dealt again, two down and two face up. Jackie's up card was a five. Vincent's up card was a seven. Her hole card was a king, and his was a six.

He looked at her. She carefully kept no expression on her face.

"I'll play these," said Jackie.

Vincent turned up one card for himself.

Ten of hearts.

Busted again.

They played all the way through the deck. Vincent never won a round.

"Maybe," he said. "*Coulda* been luck...or you coulda been counting cards or something."

Jackie said nothing, and just watched him, waiting.

"Okay, here's what we're gonna do, puss," he said, nodding to himself. "Get dressed. We're going shopping."

VINCENT STOPPED AT the first convenience store that he spotted. Jackie cringed, because she occasionally frequented this store for the kids. She had never bought lottery tickets here, because she didn't want to draw attention to herself so close to home.

"Here's what's happening," said Vincent. "You're going to do your thing with the scratch-offs. Anything with a payoff of a hundred bucks or more, we'll buy. No more than ten of each scratch-off, though...we're trying to *make* money, not *spend* all of our money. Understand?"

Jackie nodded, resigned.

"Hey, if it makes you feel better, this is the only store we'll hit today. How's that? Then you can get home in time to meet the 'tards," Vincent said cheerfully.

She looked up and glared at Vincent. A gush of protective anger flowed through her, and she said, "Don't call them that." Jackie shook her head, and said, quietly but forcefully, "Don't *ever* call them that."

Vincent was about to backhand Jackie, until he looked into her eyes. He was startled when he saw a flash of indigo there. Instead, he nodded. "Okay, Jackie. You make me money, and I'll call them whatever you want me to." He opened the car door. "Now, let's go."

Jackie looked down at the dashboard. *Where did* that *come from, Jackie?* She shook her head at herself. *Keep that up, and you'll get yourself* and *the kids killed!* She opened the car door and climbed out. *But...I'm* the one with the gift. I'm the golden goose. It's *me* they want to make money for them. So, I'll make them some money...and watch for my chance.* She and Vincent went inside the store.

Most of the time, when Jackie came to this store, she brought the children with her. The store was within walking distance for all of them, and the exercise did them all good, plus the store had a Baskin-Robbins ice cream section inside, and tables for customers to sit and eat. They would all get ice cream, eat it at the store, then walk home when they were done. Sometimes, a rainstorm would sneak up on them after they arrived...and the store manager, Steve Bell, would insist on piling all the kids into his minivan and driving them all home.

So, of course Steve was behind the counter.

Vincent was a stranger to Steve. Vincent had yet to conduct any business with this establishment...a situation that he would have to rectify soon.

As Vincent's eyes scanned the store seeking potential protection profit, Steve looked up and saw the pair. A look of concern crossed his face when he saw Vincent, but went away as he saw Jackie.

"Hi, Jackie!" said Steve. "Nice day, isn't it?"

Jackie nodded. "Sure is, Steve."

"Anything I can help you with?" he asked, glancing at Vincent.

Jackie saw the glance, and got worried. "No, Steve, I'm just here to pick up some scratch-offs. Give us a minute, would you?"

Steve nodded. "Sure. Just yell when you're ready."

"Thanks," Jackie replied. She snuck a peek at Vincent. Of course, he caught it.

He eased close to her side and whispered in her ear. "I don't like that little look. Don't do anything to get that man killed. *Capice*?"

Jackie swallowed hard to ease her fear, and nodded.

"Good. Now, do your stuff and let's get out of here," whispered Vincent.

Jackie hesitated. "How many winners do you want?"

"All of them, down to number ten in the stack."

Jackie closed her eyes and began running her fingers along the plexiglass, first one row, then the next, until she had scanned all of them. She opened her eyes and looked at Vincent.

"Get your money ready. There's several," she told him.

Vincent nodded. "I got it."

Jackie took a deep breath. "Steve, can you come over here?"

WHEN VINCENT LED JACKIE out of the store, he had spent three hundred and ninety-two dollars. Jackie had provided winners totaling five thousand, two hundred and thirty-seven dollars.

As he drove her home, Vincent thought to himself that there was no *way* his bosses were going to let her out from under their control.

Chapter 3

That night, as Jackie prepared dinner for the children, she thought over the day's events.

Vincent's last comments to her were what she remembered the most.

"Now, look," he had said. "After I leave, your first thought will probably be to tell somebody about this. The cops, maybe, or a friend. Or even the kids. Just know one thing, puss: you tell anybody, and I kill them. You tell the cops, I kill the kids. Got it?" When she indicated that she "had it", Vincent had left, saying, "I'll be back...either tomorrow or the next day. We may try the track, too. I gotta talk to my boss."

That was the moment that Jackie realized that this big jerk would never let her go back to her normal life.

She would have to come up with some way to extricate herself from this mess. Preferably something that wouldn't get anyone killed.

AFTER DINNER, THE KIDS had finished their homework. Showers were done in shifts, and nighttime was shower time for Nicky, Tommy, and Cynthia. They were all gathered in the living room. It was nine o'clock, and time for an hour of television before bed. The kids had all earned it.

It was Nicky's turn to choose what to watch, and he chose ESPN. Cynthia and Jennie Lou groaned and writhed, as if watching sports were a physical pain. Tommy grinned, and Nicky laughed out loud. Even Phillip smiled at the hammy acting put on by the girls.

Jackie smiled, and switched to ESPN. It was just in time for a news conference.

The announcer said that they were joining some guy named Bo Lockhart, a boxing promoter hosting the Championship boxing match at the convention center here in the city.

The kids were all watching. They liked keeping up with what was going on in the city, and they liked boxing...even Phillip was watching with rapt attention.

A man – presumably Bo Lockhart – came to a podium. "Ladies and gentlemen, please quiet down and take your seats. Please." Lockhart paused as the reporters sat down. "Thank you. As some of you may have heard, we had some excitement here earlier today." Several of the reporters laughed. "Well, here's what happened. One of our security people, in a sparring match with Mike Swanson, knocked out the challenger with one punch." Reporters started barking questions again. "Please, people, let me finish! We'll have time for all of your questions later! Please!" The reporters quieted down again. "In order to continue the fight as planned Tuesday night, the security man has offered to take the place of the challenger." More questions were shouted. "People, you will have your chance!" The reporters again began restraining themselves. "We accepted the man's offer, and so did the Champ. Ladies and gentlemen, I give you the new challenger: Percival 'King Louie' Washington!"

Jackie watched as a handsome, stoutly-built black man approached the podium, shook hands with Lockhart, apparently exchanged a few words, then faced the audience...while Lockhart exited the stage, shaking his right hand as if it hurt. The man began to speak.

"You know, my mama, Betty, was raised to be polite when she was comin' up in Alabama. You folks would shame her." The reporters began quieting. "There ain't no need to all shout at once. I'll answer your questions, but you got to be orderly. Everybody's gonna have a chance - won't none of you get no exclusive. So, just be calm." He pointed to a lady in the front row. "How 'bout ladies first?"

"Miriam Apple, Channel Seven news. Aren't you Louie Washington from Justice Security here in the city?"

Louie nodded. "Yes, ma'am, I am."

Wow! Justice Security! I've heard a lot about them...wonder if they could help me? thought Jackie to herself.

"What will Joey Justice and the rest of your company say about this?"

"Dey all gonna kick my broad black ass, ma'am." Laughter erupted in the auditorium. "Actually, my partners are my friends. Dey gonna be real supportive, and wish me the best. Everybody else there works *for* me, so what do *you* think they gonna say?" More laughter. Louie pointed to the man next to her. "Your turn."

"Ted Hanson, ESPN. Mr. Washington, what really happened with Mike Swanson today? In your words."

Louie took a breath. "I was tryin' to show Mr. Swanson the value of havin' bodyguards and security people. He took offense, and called me an unfortunate name. I suggested that he meet me in the ring for a sparring match to settle our differences." He paused. "I showed Mr. Swanson the error of his ways."

"How many times was Mr. Swanson able to hit you before you knocked him out?"

"Man never laid a glove on me." Reporters again all started shouting at once. Louie lost his patience. "People, *what de hell did I just say about takin' turns?*" he said loudly. Sudden silence filled the auditorium. "Thank you." He started again. "Mr. Swanson threw several punches, but none of them connected."

He pointed at the next man. "Yo' turn, man."

"Mr. Washington, why do they call you King Louie?"

Louie laughed. "'Member I told you 'bout my partners bein' my friends? We all met back in college, and one of Misty's favorite movies was *The Jungle Book*. Dey said my face resembled King Louie's. The nickname stuck, 'cause anything's better than Percy!"

Everyone laughed again. Louie pointed at the next reporter. "Go, man."

"Harold Chamberlain, *Washington Post*. Is it true that your company has several high-level, top secret contracts with the Federal government?"

Louie shook his head in disgust. "Man, I can't talk about no security business. What the hell you thinkin'?"

As they watched Washington answer several more questions, Jackie noticed that Jennie Lou and Phillip were both watching closely, while Nicky and Tommy were speculating whether Washington could beat the Champ. Cynthia was watching Nicky and Tommy, and smiling at her foster brothers.

"Hey, Phillip!" said Nicky. "Who do you think will win, man?"

Since it was a contest not just of skill, but also of chance, Jackie already knew the answer.

Phillip began rocking gently. After a moment, he said, "*Louie!*"

Jennie Lou nodded, as if confirming something to herself.

THE NEXT MORNING, MIKE Woods picked up the kids to take them to school. Looking into Jackie's eyes, he said, "You okay, Jackie?"

Seeing real concern in Mike's eyes, Jackie almost burst into tears. Quickly getting herself under control, she looked at him and said, "I'm fine, Mike...really. Just a little tired, I guess."

Nodding dubiously, Mike climbed into the bus and said to her, "You know you can count on me anytime something is wrong, don't you?"

"I know," replied Jackie. "Take care of my kids, will you?"

Mike smiled. "Always." Looking into his rear view mirror, he yelled, "Who's ready for Mikey's Magic Bus Ride?"

The kids all yelled variations of "I am!"

Still smiling, Mike closed the bus doors and began rolling them to school.

Watching them out of sight, Jackie couldn't help but feel tense. Yesterday, a stranger had been sitting at her dining table when she went back inside. She turned to return inside, praying that he would not be there today.

THE "STRANGER" IN QUESTION, Vincent, was just sitting down to a breakfast meeting with his boss, Leo Lesko.

The two men were eating at a small diner on Second Avenue often frequented by the Giambini "family".

Leo arose from his booth as Vincent came closer, and the two men hugged, then sat down. Vincent ordered a light breakfast from the man who appeared at his side.

"It's good to see you, Vincent," said Lesko.

"It's really good to see you, too, boss."

"So what can I do for you today, Vincent? You said it was kinda urgent."

Vincent looked at his boss. "Mr. Lesko, I took four hundred bucks off the top of the protection money and spent it."

Lesko gave Vincent a hard look. "I hope you have a good reason for that, Vincent."

"I spent it on lottery tickets."

Lesko just looked at Vincent with no expression on his face.

"I won fifty two hundred dollars, and put it all in the bag."

Lesko's eyes widened at this news. "Well, that's great, Vincent. But we can't have our people taking from the till and spending it on lottery tickets whenever they want. What if you'd lost? It's bad for you, and bad for business."

Vincent smiled at his boss. "I wasn't worried."

"And why not?"

"I found the mother lode, Mr. Lesko," said Vincent, and told Lesko all about Jackie Blue.

Lesko thought for a moment, and said, "Vincent."

"Sir?"

"We gotta go see Mickey Giambini. He's gotta hear about this."

JACKIE WAS SO PREOCCUPIED with her fear that Vincent would show back up that she didn't get anything accomplished that day. She wandered the house like a zombie.

She sat down at the dining table. After a few minutes, she moved to the living room and turned on the television. Then she decided to change the bed linens, but got distracted after she went upstairs. Wandering back downstairs, she intended to start some kind of dinner...but couldn't make a decision as to what to make.

Jackie tossed several ideas through her head that might get her out of her predicament. Each one was dismissed when she realized that none would keep her or the kids from getting killed.

Jackie realized that she was alone against the mob, with no way out.

Jacqueline Belew, the lady that always won, had never felt so defeated in her life.

MICKEY GIAMBINI HAD an office on the fifth floor of the Crosselli Import/Export building. Of course, the Crosselli Import/Export business was a front for the family business. Business was conducted throughout the building, but family business was only conducted on the fifth floor, because Giambini had the entire floor swept for electronic eavesdropping devices twice a day. Sentries patrolled the roof, and were also placed in fixed visual observation posts in order to lessen the chances of the FBI placing infrared visual devices or long-distance listening devices in the surrounding buildings. Chances were slim that the FBI would be able to infiltrate any of the surrounding buildings, because the Giamabini family owned most of them, and the ones that weren't owned by the family had owners that would suddenly disappear should their buildings become occupied by law enforcement.

Seated in the ornate visitor chairs in front of Giambini's expansive imported desk, Vincent tried not to be intimidated. He had been a poor neighborhood kid, and the sight of all this opulence triggered feelings of not being good enough. An office that was meant to be relaxing, for him, had the opposite effect.

Beside him, Lesko sat in one of the other visitor chairs. Lesko was comfortable.

Across the desk, Mickey Giambini sat, flanked by a bodyguard.

"Leo! Vincent!" said Giambini. "It's good to see you. What's so urgent with you guys?"

Leo spoke. "Mickey, thank you for seeing us so quickly. We got kind of a situation here that I never seen before. We need some...advice...on how to handle it. Vincent here will tell you all about it."

Mickey Giambini had once broken the neck of a whore's newborn before beating her within an inch of her life for costing him more money than she made. The only reason he didn't kill her was so that she could earn him back the money she had cost by being out of commission for birthing a baby. He had killed so many men in his rise to the top of the mob family that even *he* had lost count. Many had been killed for no more reason than a suspicion of wrongdoing. Proof was not a requirement in Mickey Giambini's mind. This cold-blooded man turned his attention to Vincent. Vincent almost squirmed when those steely blue eyes looked at him, but he began speaking to Giambini.

He started with his first observation of Jackie, then wrapped it up with the five thousand dollar windfall.

Mickey kept looking at Vincent, as if he were waiting for something more. Then he leaned back in his desk chair and looked at nothing for several minutes. He abruptly sat up and looked at both Vincent and Leo.

"So, whaddaya think? Is she some kind of psychic or somethin'?" he asked the two men.

"I can't say, Mickey," replied Leo. "I've never seen her. Vincent here is her only contact."

Vincent shook his head. "If she isn't, Mr. Giambini, she's a great guesser."

Giambini stared at his desktop for a moment, then slapped his hand on the top. Vincent jumped, but Lesko made no move at all.

"Okay," said Mickey Giambini. "Here's what we're gonna do. Tomorrow morning, we pick up this Jackie Belew. You two," he said, indicating Vincent and Leo Lesko, "myself, and Rizzo, here." He pointed at his bodyguard. "We'll pick places at random for this bitch to win us some money, then we go to the track. Then we'll know one way or the other, right?"

Vincent and Leo nodded. Rizzo just stood still, looking tough.

Vincent fleetingly thought he could take Rizzo, if he had to.

"All right, then," said Mickey. "We pick her up at eight in the morning."

"Tomorrow's Saturday, Mickey," said Leo. "If what Vincent says is true, the house is gonna be full of kids."

"I don't much give a shit," replied the mob boss. "We go anyway. Fuck 'em!"

THAT NIGHT, DINNER was grilled cheese sandwiches and chips. However, at the table, the kids couldn't help but notice how distracted Jackie was acting. She didn't seem to have a lot of appetite, and she mostly just pushed her food around her plate. The children kept cutting their eyes around the table to each other, until, Phillip began rocking back and forth. Nicky, Tommy, and Cynthia finally caught Jennie Lou's eyes, and each nodded.

"Jackie," said Jennie Lou.

Jackie jumped, startled. She looked around and realized that the children were looking at her, and that Phillip's rocking was becoming more rapid. "I'm sorry, Jennie Lou. I have some stuff on my mind, and I'm not very good company tonight."

"Have we done something?" asked Cynthia, quietly.

Jackie looked at Cynthia, then each child in turn. "*No*," she said emphatically. "Never. It's nothing for any of you to worry about, I promise."

Jennie said, "Are you sure we can't help?"

Jackie shook her head. "No, Jen…it's one that I have to fix all by myself."

"But you always tell us that we have to work on problems like a family. Together," said Tommy. "That means we're sposed to help you, Jackie."

"Yeah, we don't like seeing you like this," said Nicky.

"Let us help. Please?" said Cynthia.

"At least tell us what it is," agreed Jennie Lou. "Maybe we can think of something you've missed."

Phillip's rocking slowed, and he said, "Help Jackie Blue."

As Jackie listened to each child, she stared down at the table. Tears came to her eyes. "I'm sorry, kids. You're right. Most problems can be tackled together. But not this one. I have to face this one alone." She looked around the table. "I love you all soooo much. Thank you." She wiped her eyes with the backs of her hands. "So, what are we doing tomorrow?"

Cries of "baseball game" and "amusement park" were ruled out for lack of funds. It was finally decided that the zoo would be a perfect Saturday outing. Jackie went to phone Mike Woods to see if he would be willing to earn a few extra dollars for providing their transportation.

AT SEVEN FIFTY-EIGHT Saturday morning, a black limousine stopped at the curb in front of the Belew house. Vincent got out of the back and walked up the sidewalk to the front porch. After ringing the bell, he stood with his hands behind his back, waiting. The door opened, and a young boy was there.

"Can I help you?" asked the boy.

Vincent looked at the boy and said, "I'm looking for Jackie."

The boy said, "Just a minute." He shut the door, and Vincent heard, "Jackie! Some guy at the door for you!"

After a moment, the door opened again, and Jackie looked out and was shocked to see Vincent there.

"Hello, puss," said Vincent.

The door opened wider, and the same boy, Tommy, that had answered the door was there again, glaring at Vincent.

"What do you want?" asked Jackie coldly.

Vincent smiled at her anger. "I got a couple of my bosses that want to see what you can do. We need you to come along for a while."

Jackie shook her head. "I can't. I'm taking the kids to the zoo today."

Vincent shook his head with a fake look of concern. "Nope...sorry. You're coming out with us. That's the way it is."

Tommy said, "Mister, who are you?"

Vincent looked down at Tommy and said, "Shut up, crip. This is between the puss and me."

A look of anger swept Tommy's face. With an inarticulate grunt, he swung his fist at Vincent. Vincent caught the boy's small fist, registered Tommy's look of surprise, then pushed on the boy's fist and arm hard enough that Tommy fell backwards to the floor. Jackie went to Tommy to make sure he wasn't hurt, and the other children swarmed to the foyer, with Phillip in the lead.

Vincent drew his gun and pointed it at the big boy. "Come on, 'tard. One step closer."

Jackie put out her hand to Phillip in a "stop" gesture, and shouted, "Phillip! NO!"

The boy stopped. He and Vincent were the same height, but the boy was wider in the shoulders, and more muscular. Vincent realized that if he hadn't pulled the gun, the boy would have had a good chance of hurting him.

Jackie looked at Vincent and said, "Put that away, you ass. Big, tough mob man, scared of a bunch of children." To the children she said, "Kids, get Mr. Mike to take you to the zoo. I have to go with this man for a while. I'll see you tonight, okay?" She grabbed her purse and stormed past Vincent to the limousine.

Vincent smiled coldly at the children, and closed the door while making a "shooting" gesture with his thumb and forefinger.

As he approached the limo, he could hear Jackie really giving it to the men inside. When he opened the door, he heard her say, "...you might as well kill me now! If anyone threatens or harms those children again, there won't be any more lottery money for you crooks!"

Vincent shut the limo door and pulled his hand back to backslap Jackie, but Mickey Giambini said, "Vincent." Vincent put down his hand. *Lucky bitch.*

"Miss Belew, I apologize for Vincent's...enthusiasm," said Giambini, with no feeling behind the words. "I think he just wants to make sure that you play along with us for now. He meant no insult, and he will apologize to the kids right now if you want him to."

Jackie shook her head. "I don't want him *near* the children again. You can threaten me all you want, but if I see him anywhere near those children again, I don't play your game anymore, and I go to the police...or somebody!" she said disgustingly. "Am I understood? I'm willing to play for you...as long as those children are left alone!" She glared at each of the men as if daring them to contradict her wishes. "And one more thing: no more showing up at the last minute and telling me to leave. I have a houseful of special needs children, and I have to arrange that someone is there to care for them when I'm not home."

Nonplussed, Mickey Giambini replied, "Sure, Miss Belew. We'll start calling ahead. And Vincent won't go near the children again. You have my word of honor on record."

"Thank you, sir," Jackie replied. "And what is your name? And your friend's name?"

Giambini found himself complying with Jackie's request. "My name is Mickey Giambini. This is Leo Lesko. And you've met Vincent Lambosa."

Jackie kept her face calm as she heard Giambini's name. Inside, she turned cold as ice while his stomach dropped somewhere below her knees. *This is the head honcho! I'm really in for it now!*

"So why am I in a car with you this morning instead of on my way to the zoo with my kids?"

Giambini folded his hands. "Vincent says that you can...," he waved his hands expansively, "ascertain winning numbers. Mr. Lesko and I wanted to confirm this with you, and perhaps see a demonstration."

Jackie frowned a bit. "It's true. I have a gift that I've had since I can remember."

"So what's this gift? And what does it do?"

Jackie couldn't think of a reason not to open up about it, since these men weren't going away. "As I was growing up, I realized that I knew how to win any game of chance, or I could predict the winner of any game of chance. It's like I can sense it, deep inside, without any effort at all. For me, it's a natural thing...like being able to play music that you've never seen...that you've only heard once in your life. I've never been wrong, even with all the times I've tested it. I can hear what teams are playing in a baseball game, and I know who will win. I run my hand along the plastic box that holds scratch-off lottery tickets, and I know where the winners are...and how much. Or I can go to the track, and I know which horses are going to win...sometimes I get lucky and hit a long shot. The kids and I were watching a press conference about boxing the other night - the Champ is fighting one of the people from Justice Security - and I know who will win." She stopped for a moment, glanced at Vincent, then looked back at Giambini. "I've never been caught by anyone before...just bad luck that your meatheaded thug noticed me."

"So...why aren't you a millionaire?" asked Giambini. "I mean, if you can do all that, you could have done what we're asking you to do. You could have a fortune."

Jackie shook her head. "I couldn't. I feel like using it for personal gain is abusing it. I use it only when I need extra money to take care of the children. That isn't for personal gain, that is helping others with my gift. I feel that I'm allowed to do that."

Giambini looked confused. "What do you mean, 'allowed'? Who's stopping you?"

Jackie shrugged. "My conscience. Karma. God. You name it. I feel that if I use it for personal gain, I'll lose it. I don't want to lose it. I may need it sometime."

AFTER VINCENT CLOSED the front door, Jennie Lou took command.

"Okay," she said. "Phillip, would you please help Tommy out of the floor?"

She turned to look at Phillip and saw anger in his eyes. She had never seen that before.

"Never mind, Phillip," she said soothingly. "It's okay. I'm sure Jackie will be fine. Please help our little brother out of the floor. His braces are keeping him from standing. Please?"

Phillip continued staring at the front door, with no indication that he heard her. His eyes showed a deep and seething anger.

"*Phillip!*" said Jennie Lou sharply. *"Look at me! Now!"*

Phillip jumped as if startled and turned to Jennie Lou. His eyes softened immediately.

"I understand and sympathize with your anger, brother," she said calmly. "But, right now, your family needs you. Please help Tommy, okay?"

Phillip nodded and moved to his foster brother. Nicky and Cynthia, who had been standing beside Tommy, moved out of Phillip's way. Phillip reached down and gently picked Tommy up and stood him upright, holding the younger boy under his arms.

Tommy turned to Phillip and hugged the bigger boy. "Thanks, Phillip!"

Phillip began to slowly rock back and forth.

Cynthia said, "Jen, who was that mean man?"

"Yeah, and what did he want with Jackie?" asked Nicky.

Jennie Lou maneuvered her wheelchair so that she faced her foster siblings. "I don't know, guys. We're going to have to ask Jackie a lot of questions later."

The others thought for a moment, then either said "no" or shook their heads.

"But should we call the police, Jennie Lou?" asked Cynthia.

"I'm more scared of the police than I am that man with the gun," said Nicky.

"I think we should call them. That man would have shot Phillip!" Tommy said.

Jennie Lou thought for a moment, then said, "And if the police called Children's Services? And they decided to take us away from Jackie? Or separated us?"

Everyone looked very somber.

"I don't want to lose Jackie, and I don't want to lose you. For the first time since my accident, I feel like I've got a real family, and I will *not* give it up! So, the police are out of this. Are we agreed?"

The children all nodded, except Phillip. He only rocked back and forth gently.

"Okay, so that's settled. Now, we've got some things we have to make decisions about...Mr. Mike will be here in less than an hour. I don't think Jackie would want us to tell him about this, do you? What do we tell him about Jackie not being here today? And not going to the zoo with us today?"

The other children looked confused and scared. No one spoke.

"LET'S HOPE THAT YOU don't lose it," said Giambini. "That would be detrimental to our relationship. I would have to ask Vincent to perform certain...unpleasant...duties if that happened."

Jackie rolled her eyes. "Look, I got it. You're the mob, or Mafia, or family business, or whatever, and you want me to use my talent to make you money, or you're gonna kill me...or kill the kids...or kill whoever. Yada, yada, yada...Big deal." She leaned forward, bringing her closer to Giambini. "I think you rely on threats far too much. Why not try the carrot-and-stick approach? Offer something that can help me in return for the incoming cash flow? Help me with taking care of the kids?" She leaned back as she spread her hands. "*That's* the way to get me to work for you. After all, it's what I do it for anyway."

Giambini looked at Jacqueline. "Look, *Miss Belew*. Let's get something straight between you and me." He leaned in close to Jackie, eyes blazing hard anger toward her. "I ain't doin' a fuckin' thing for no crips, no retards, and no piece of fluff...except to let you stay alive long enough to make me some money. I believe that is both the carrot *and* the stick...correct?" He leaned back. "Are we clear on this point, *Miss Belew*?"

Vincent and Lesko chuckled, while Jackie both grew cold with fear and determined with anger. The threat from Giambini was the deciding factor in what Jackie knew she had to do.

If she could stay alive long enough to do it, that is.

MIKE WOODS STOPPED at the curb of Jackie's house on Peach Street and got out of his privately owned, specially designed van.

When Jackie had called last night to ask if he was free to ferry her and the kids to the zoo today, he had been secretly elated. He loved the kids, and had found himself falling deeply in love with Jackie, too. So, naturally, he said he would be delighted to take them.

Each day, Mike told himself that today would be the day he gathered enough courage to tell Jacqueline Belew that he loved her.

And, each day, he wasn't able to do it.

No matter how much he cajoled himself, or threatened himself, or told himself that if he didn't act, he would lose his opportunity with her to some other guy that *had* the courage.

Mike kicked himself for that particular shortcoming often. He didn't have a problem telling the kids that he loved them. But, with Jackie...

He would look into those eyes...he had often seen the sunset reflected in them, because of the school schedules for the kids, and the traffic problems in the city. He longed to see the sunrise there.

And he knew that time was slipping away, like sifting sand...Maybe today was the day...

He knocked on the front door with a big smile on his face.

CHOOSING A CONVENIENCE store at random, Giambini explained what was going to happen.

"You and Vincent will go in and you will do what you do. Leo and I will watch. Easy cheesy, right, Miss Belew?"

Jackie nodded.

Giambini nodded back, and everyone got out of the limousine.

Inside the store, Jackie went immediately to the plexiglass cabinet containing the scratch-off lottery tickets. She closed her eyes and ran her hand along each row of the cabinet. *Just like a trained monkey in a circus. Oh, God, if you're listening, please watch over this poor fool that I am!* When she finished, she gave Vincent the list of winners. Not that many in this store today.

Once Vincent bought what she told him to buy, the four people went back to the limo to scratch off the tickets. Cash outlay had been three hundred and forty-seven dollars. Cash return was one thousand eleven dollars.

"Not a bad haul," said Giambini.

"Mr. Giambini, you see what I told you," said Vincent.

Giambini nodded. "Yeah...yeah, Vincent, I see." He looked at Jackie. "Baseball game this afternoon between the city's team and the Cubs. Who wins?"

"Cubs, three to two."

Giambini motioned to Rizzo. "Go bet five large on the Cubs to win three to two. Get odds if you can." Rizzo pulled out a cell phone and walked a few feet away. Giambini looked at Jackie. "You better be right, or that five grand is coming out of your ass...in trade."

Jackie swallowed. There it was. It always came down to sex of some kind with people like these...a kind of 'my dick's bigger than yours' or 'you ain't got a dick, so I'm gonna screw you' thing. To Giambini, she replied, "Well, at least that's one worry I won't have. You'll win. Guaranteed." *But you just wait...I'm going to cost you a fortune, you arrogant pizza peddler.*

Giambini nodded. "Okay, let's take this dough to the track and let Miss Jackie turn it into more."

Everyone piled back into the limo, and Rizzo drove them toward the race track. Jackie Blue prayed the winning horses would be long shots today. It would make the fall, when it came, even better.

"SO JACKIE WENT TO TAKE care of her sick brother this morning?" asked Mike Woods.

Four kids nodded. Phillip rocked back and forth.

"And she left about forty-five minutes ago? And wanted me to take you kids to the zoo without her?"

Four kids nodded. Phillip rocked back and forth.

Mike looked at the kids. "You guys are lying," he said simply.

Protest cries came from four of the kids.

Mike held up his hand, palm out. When they had quieted down, Mike looked at Jennie Lou. "Jen, you have *never* lied to me before. What is going on?"

Jennie Lou was quiet, and would not meet Mike's eyes.

"I'm telling you all that we are not going anywhere until you tell me what is happening, and where Jacqueline is," said Mike.

Silence from the children.

"I'll call the cops if I have to...I'll file a missing persons report."

"No!" yelled Nicky, Tommy, and Cynthia together.

"Ha!" said Mike. "Now we're gettin' somewhere." He looked hard at the younger children. "Tell. Me. Now."

The three youngest children looked at each other, the ground, and passed quick guilty glances at both Mike and Jennie Lou.

"Oh, all right," said Jennie Lou. "It's pretty obvious that the little ones are going to spill it anyway. Phillip, would you please push my chair a little closer to the table?" He did so. "Thank you." She took a deep breath and let it out. "Okay, Mr. Mike. This morning, a man came to the front door...none of us kids had ever seen him before..."

WHEN THE GROUP ARRIVED at the racetrack, all five people climbed out of the limousine. Jackie led the entourage, followed by the four men. She was thinking.

I look like some rock star or something, with a bunch of big, bad men guarding me. If that were the case, I wouldn't be quite as worried as I am now. Maybe I can go home once the races are over for the day. And I hope the kids are okay! I know this morning terrified them!

Vincent bought a racing form listing all of the races, and all of the horses in each race. He looked it over, then handed it to Lesko. Lesko and Giambini looked it over, too.

"Okay, Miss Belew," said Giambini. "Here's a list of today's races. I want win, place, and show for each race."

Jackie took the paper. *Pet monkey performs again...but I don't even get a banana.* She ran her hand down each race, naming the horses in each race for first, second, and third places: win, place, and show. There weren't any long shot winners today, Jackie told them. The best odds were going to be five-to-one in the third race. Vincent took the lottery money to the betting windows and placed bets for the first race.

"SO, JACKIE LEFT WITH this guy," said Mike Woods, "and he was going to shoot Phillip?"

The kids all nodded.

"But she acted like she knew him?"

More nods.

"Sounds suspicious to me," said Mike. "Trouble is, if we call the police, it could make things worse...at least, until we talk to Jackie and find out what's what. For all we know, it could be nothing, and the guy could have been playing a big joke on everyone."

Cynthia went over to Mike and sat on his knee. "Mr. Mike, do you really believe that?"

Mike opened his mouth to speak, then closed it again. Looking into Cynthia's eyes, there was no way he could lie to her. "No, Cindy-Windy, I don't." He looked at Phillip, still gently rocking, and at each other kid in turn. "I think she's in trouble, and it sounds pretty deep. She needs our help, whether she wants it or not, and when she gets here, we'll ask her about it. Meanwhile, it's getting on toward lunch time. Show me where the grub is, and I'll cook us all up something filling." He stood Cynthia up, then stood himself. "After we eat, I'll whip each and every one of you with a game of cards. How's that sound, ya buncha rats?"

It was agreeable to the children. Mr. Mike, true to his word, won every game with them.

"I DON'T FUCKIN' BELIEVE it!" shouted Mickey Giambini as the winning horse in the last race crossed the finish line. He whirled around to Jackie with a huge smile on his face. "Do you know how much we cleared today? And it was all thanks to *you!*"

"I told you, Mr. Giambini," said Vincent. "This puss can keep us in money forever!"

"I'm beginning to believe that, Vincent," replied Giambini. He turned to Rizzo. "Call and find out if the baseball game is over. What odds did you get on the Cubs?"

"Three to one, boss," replied Rizzo, as he dialed the phone.

While Rizzo was on the phone, Giambini was still singing Jackie's praises to Vincent and to Lesko. "I never believed in that ESP crap before...now it's slappin' me right in the face!" He shook his head in disbelief. "I been worried about that fuckin' Fernandez comin' in and takin' over everything...worryin' about where the replacement money was gonna come from if I had to give up the drugs because of that Mexican fruitcake! And here's the answer," he gestured to Jackie, "one pretty little woman. I still don't fuckin' believe it!"

Rizzo snapped his phone shut. "Cubs won, boss. We won fifteen grand."

Giambini stared at Rizzo with his mouth open, momentarily speechless. He turned to Jackie, eyes wide, and said, "Holy crap...Miss Belew, you're a saint."

Rizzo's phone rang again. He took it out and listened for a few moments. He looked at Giambini and said, "Boss. Gucci and Romano just got back from their meeting with Fernandez. They delivered the fireworks as arranged."

Giambini shook his head. "I got one piece of advice for all of you. Stay away from the convention center Tuesday night. Fernandez really has a hard on for that Justice Security bunch." He thought for a minute, and turned to Jackie. "Hold on a minute...didn't you say you knew who would win that Championship fight Tuesday night?"

Jackie nodded.

"So who's gonna win?"

"Washington," she said. "The one they call 'King Louie.'"

"Sweet Mary-Mother-Of-God," said Giambini. He looked at Lesko. "Do you know what the odds are that one measly security guard will beat the Heavyweight Champion of the world?" He turned to Rizzo. "What were the odds this morning?"

"Twenty-to-one, boss."

"Holy cow!" said Giambini. "We gotta go back to the office. I gotta see how much cash we got on hand." He motioned to Jackie. "Let's take this blessed lady back home. If this thing with the boxing match comes through, we won't ever need to bother Jacqueline Belew again...for a while, anyway."

LATER, THE LIMO DREW to a stop in front of Jackie's house. Before she opened the door to get out, Giambini stopped her.

"We may come back, if something happens," he said. "Or, if cash reserves run low, we'll come back and get you to find more for us. For now, though, thank you. You have my respect, Miss Belew."

Jackie nodded at him and climbed out of the car. As she walked up the sidewalk, she could hear the limousine driving away behind her. She couldn't help but feel that a bullet was going to pop into her back as she walked away.

But, it didn't.

As she reached her front door, it opened before she could touch it. Mike Woods and five anxious children were there, waiting for her.

Jacqueline Belew burst into tears as she crossed the threshold and was wrapped in the arms, both large and small, of the people that loved her.

Chapter 4

"**I**s that why you won't play games with us?" Tommy asked.

Jackie nodded. "That's why. I always know what to do to win, and it takes the fun out of it. I'd rather watch you guys play and have fun."

"Are those bad men coming back, Jackie?" asked Nicky.

"Not for a while, Nicky. Hopefully, never again."

"I bet Mr. Mike could kick that man's behind," said Cynthia.

"Well, I dunno about *that,*" said Mike. "I'd sure like the chance, though."

"No!" said Jackie quickly. "That man is dangerous! And crazy! It's like he doesn't care what he does, or who he does it to!" She took Mike's hand. "*Promise me you'll stay away from him! Promise me now, Mike!*"

Mike, surprised at the passion in Jackie's voice and the fear in her eyes, hurriedly said, "Sure, Jackie! I promise! If it means that much to you, I'll stay away from him."

Nicky, Tommy, and Cynthia looked knowingly at Jennie Lou, who winked at the younger children.

"You know, Jackie," said Jennie Lou, "I think Mr. Mike will make *somebody* a wonderful husband..."

Picking up on Jennie Lou's hint, Cynthia chimed in. "Yeah, he'd be a great husband!"

Tommy said, "And a great dad..."

"And a built-in bus driver," said Nicky.

Phillip spoke. "*Great* dad!"

Jackie and Mike were both blushing beet red.

"I gotta say something," said Mike. He turned to Jackie. "I been wanting to say this for a long time, Jackie. I...uh...," he stammered. "Dang it! I been in love with you for a long time, Jackie. I want nothin' more than to be your man, and a good daddy to these kids." He took a deep breath. "Wow. That wasn't so bad." He laughed nervously.

Jackie was looking at her hands, twisting together nervously in her lap. It was now or never. She looked up into his eyes. "You are a good man, Mike Woods, and so gentle and patient with these kids. You're don't seem to be after anything, or have any ulterior motives, and that has totally captured my heart. I've been in love with you, too...and still am. I would be honored to be with you."

Mike took Jackie gently by the shoulders. "Then, I guess we're together." He looked into her eyes. "I guess I should kiss you now."

Jackie nodded. "I guess you should."

So he did.

When the kiss was over, both adults looked at the children. Four of them were staring, mouths wide open in surprise. Phillip, however, was smiling.

Jackie giggled. "Close your mouths, children. You'll catch flies."

The children tackled the two adults, and covered them with hugs.

"SO, THAT'S EVERY PENNY we can scrounge up?" asked Mickey Giambini.

Giambini's accountant nodded. "That's every penny, Mr. Giambini. Eighteen million, three hundred ninety-seven thousand, four hundred twenty-two dollars."

Giambini looked at Rizzo. "Call them. Bet the whole thing on Louie Washington to win."

The accountant squirmed. "Mr. Giambini, I strongly recommend against this. If you should lose, we won't have any cash at all, and we won't be able to..."

"We're betting it. Every penny," interrupted Giambini. "We got a sure thing here! Esteban Fernandez is gonna blow the convention center as soon as the winner of the fight is announced. Washington is gonna win the fight. It's a sure thing! Once that center blows, there won't be any question about who the winner is! And with twenty-to-one odds, that's over three hundred and sixty-seven million dollars we put into our pockets...and if that crazy Mexican keeps trying to come into the city, we're gonna need it for keeping him off our turf. So, yeah, we're betting every penny we got. *Capice?*"

The accountant nodded. "Yes, Mr. Giambini. But you know part of my job is to warn you when I think something is financially risky. You'd be mad at me if I didn't."

"You're right, and you done your job just right," replied Giambini. "This time it's okay. Now get outta here!"

The accountant left.

"Vincent," said Giambini.

"Yes, sir," replied Vincent.

"You're the one that found that Belew woman, right?"

"Yes, sir."

"You're promoted, as of right now. In this family business, there's me, then there's Leo and you. You're both equal, and you both answer only to me."

Vincent was stunned. "*Thank* you, Mr. Giambini!"

"Hey, you earned it!"

JACKIE, MIKE, AND THE kids were gathered around the dinner table on Sunday, discussing the Giambini situation again.

"So, Giambini said something was going to happen at the convention center Tuesday night?" asked Mike.

"Yes."

"And it involved 'fireworks'?"

Jackie nodded. "And somebody named Fernandez. Giambini said that this Fernandez 'really had a hard on for this Justice Security'. Wonder if he's going to try to blow up the convention center?"

"Nobody's that crazy," said Mike. "But we'll stay home and watch the fight on pay-per-view anyway."

Nicky yelled, "Yay!"

Everyone's plate was full, and the dish passing stopped. Jackie said, "Mike, will you say grace, please?"

Taken by surprise, Mike said, "Sure, Jackie."

Everyone held hands and bowed their heads.

"Lord, please smile down on us, and favor us with your blessings. Together, the seven of us can face anything, and will be a force to contend with, as long as you are behind us. Thank you for the blessings that are these children, and thank you for the blessing that is Jacqueline Belew. Please bless this food, and the hands that prepared it. In Jesus' name...Amen."

"Okay, kids, dig in!" finished Mike.

"May I say one thing?" asked Jackie. Everyone looked at her. "Just in case, if anything happens to me, here's what I want you to do, and I don't want any arguments about it."

And she told them.

"OKAY, BOSS," SAID RIZZO. "Our friends in Vegas says they got the whole amount covered. They also said you might not be running on all your cylinders by betting on that security guard."

Mickey Giambini chuckled. "Let 'em think it. They'll think something else when that security guard wins that boxing match!"

THE REST OF SUNDAY, all of Monday, and most of Tuesday were quiet, normal days for Jackie. When Mike Woods arrived with the children after school, he stayed to have dinner and to watch the fight on television.

At seven forty-five, the television was turned to the pay-per-view channel, and everyone was gathered around to watch. Nicky, especially, was very excited about the match.

"I like the champ," he told everyone. "But the more I heard about King Louie, the more I'm hoping he'll win. And he lives here *in the city!* One of us could actually *meet* him!"

"You *wish*, gooberhead," said Tommy, and hit Nicky with a pillow.

The two boys began wrestling on the living room floor. Mike was laughing, Cynthia was trying not to get in their way, and even Jackie was smiling.

"Phillip," said Jackie. "Would you separate those two before they destroy the living room, please?"

Phillip, a slight smile on his face, bent at the waist and grabbed each boy by the back of the pants and lifted them, seemingly with no effort at all. The boys were giggling and saying, "Hey!" and "Put us down, Phillip!"

Jackie asked them, "Are you two going to behave?"

Both boys nodded.

"Okay, Phillip. Please put them down...*gently!*"

Phillip did, then returned to his seat.

Jennie Lou said quietly, "Boys, the fight is starting."

Everyone turned to the television. The announcer was just introducing Louie. On the screen, the camera zoomed in on Louie's corner. There were three men there. The television announcer said that the second man was Dexter Beck and the third man was Turk Wendall, also of Justice Security. There was scattered catcalls, applause, and even a few "boos" here and there.

As soon as the three had reached the designated corner, the announcer began the litany again for the champ.

"And now, without further delay, here he is. Weighing in at 254 pounds, it's the heavyweight champion of the world! Ladies and gentlemen, Walter Pyle!"

The champ had no compunctions against showing off for the crowd. Through the tumultuous applause, Pyle danced down the aisle to the ring, both arms in the air, throwing punches to the rooftop. His seconds followed, big smiles on their faces. Pyle weaved back and forth across the aisle as he danced, giving a big hug to one female fan. He crossed the aisle and dry-humped another female fan. The audience apparently loved Pyle's antics, because they applauded even harder at this.

The camera cut to Louie. He was watching with narrowed eyes. It was the only expression showing on his face. He motioned for the man the announcer had said was Dexter Beck to move closer to him. He made some comments to his friend. Dexter laughed, then whispered into the ear of the one called Turk. Then both men laughed.

The younger boys were laughing at the champ. Jackie quickly corrected their admiration.

"Boys, that is nothing to be applauding about," she said. "It's very demeaning to those women, and I will not have a child in this house disrespecting someone else. Is that clear?"

Both boys nodded, wide-eyed.

Finally, the champ had moved into his own corner of the ring. He sat down on the stool and stared across the ring at Louie.

The applause had begun to die down when the referee climbed into the ring. It began again, although not as boisterously. A few boos and catcalls could be heard as well. The referee stepped to the center of the ring. He motioned to both Louie and the champ to come to the center of the ring with him. Both complied. When they moved to the referee, the referee clicked a button on a wireless microphone on his shirt.

"Pyle, Washington, I want a good, clean fight. No hitting below the belt, no biting, no stomping of the other man's feet. When I say to break out of a clinch, do it, and go to a neutral corner. Is that clear, gentlemen?" Both men nodded. "Then go to your corners. When the bell sounds, come out fighting!"

The referee turned his microphone off. Both fighters continued standing in the center of the ring. Pyle spoke to Louie, then Louie spoke back...and smiled.

As Louie went back to his corner, another man was there.

The television announcer said that the man was Joey Justice, and that he must be giving his friend some last minute advice. The family saw Louie pull Joey close to him and speak, then, after a moment, he let Joey go. Joey then trotted up the aisle, with the man named Turk following.

"I wonder what's going on?" asked Jennie Lou speculatively.

"I'm guessing that they know something is going to happen tonight," said Jackie.

"Yeah, I bet you're right," said Mike.

Both boxers toed the mark, and the bell rang for the first round. Pyle threw a right at Louie's nose that almost caught him. Louie dodged the punch, but it was close. If Pyle was surprised, he didn't show it. He followed the piston-like right with a left uppercut that again barely missed Louie's chin. However, the champ left an opening, and Louie took it. He hit Pyle with a right to the side of the head. Hard.

Pyle shook his head. The punch had shaken him.

"*YES!*" shouted Nicky, as he punched the air above his head. He turned around, excited. "Did you guys *see* that punch? Fan-*tas*-tic!"

"DID YOU BUMS *see* that punch? Fan-*tas*-tic!" shouted Mickey Giambini.

Rizzo smiled and nodded. Lesko smiled. Vincent was watching his boss. For some reason, when his boss shouted, it made him nervous.

They continued watching the fight.

JACKIE AND MIKE SMILED at Nicky's enthusiasm.

On the screen, Pyle threw several more punches at Louie, who dodged each one.

The bell sounded the end of the first round. The only punch that had connected had been Louie's. He walked to his corner, and sat on the stool that the man called Dexter had put there.

"Man!" said Nicky. "The champ hasn't laid a finger on King Louie!"

"I have a question," said Jennie Lou. "Why didn't this Louie guy follow up on his punch earlier? He had a perfect setup, and could've taken out the Champ."

"I think he knows that, honey," said Mike. "I think Joey Justice told him to delay things if he could, and if he finishes off the Champ early, they can't stop what this bad guy wants to do tonight."

"Why does that bad guy want to hurt people?" asked Cynthia.

Jackie fielded that question. "Some people believe that if they hurt others, it earns them respect. They think that hurt makes them something bigger or better than everyone else. Usually, all it does is make people afraid...until they fight back, and stop the hurting."

"Hey, the fight's about to start again," said Tommy, pointing at the screen.

On the television screen, Louie stood to go toe the mark, talking over his shoulder to his friend. When the bell rang, he started to turn toward the ring. Pyle was already there, and landed a haymaker punch on the left side of Louie's face. Pyle followed with one-two punches to Louie's kidneys. When Louie spun to face the champ, Pyle punched Louie hard on the right side of his head. Louie staggered a bit, then fell to the floor of the ring, face down and barely concious.

The referee was counting.

Jackie's stomach turned to ice. Had her gift finally failed her?

"WHAT THE *fuck* is this?" yelled Giambini at the top of his lungs. His stomach had turned to ice. What was he thinking, betting all his cash on this nobody? "If he don't get up, Jackie Belew lays down with him!" He whirled to Rizzo. "*Capice?*"

"Come on, get *up!*" yelled Nicky to the television. "I believe in you, King Louie! *Please* get up!"

On the screen, the referee had counted to three, and Louie had pushed up to his hands and knees. By the time the ref counted six, Louie stood up. He nodded to the ref, who waved Pyle back into the match. Louie glared at Pyle with unblinking eyes under lowered brows. He looked really angry.

Louie feinted with a right, then followed through with a piston-like hard punch to the face with his left. The champ ducked slightly, so he didn't receive the full effect of the punch, but it still shook Pyle to the core of his being. When Louie followed through with a hard right to the stomach, Pyle bent slightly from the punch, but Louie didn't let up. He punched the same spot on Pyle's stomach with his left. Pyle hunched over even lower. Louie reached back with his right arm, and hit the side of Pyle's face with everything he had. The punch actually lifted Pyle off of the floor of the ring, spun him around, and flung him into the ropes. Slowly he slipped from the ropes onto the floor of the ring, for a count of ten.

Percival "King Louie" Washington had just become the Heavyweight Champion of the World.

And the crowd went wild.

And Louie closed his eyes and put his arms over his head.

And the children all yelled and whistled, happy that Louie had won the fight.

And Jacqueline Belew's heart started beating again.

MICKEY GIAMBINI AND his people just stared at the screen, mouths open and moving, but no sounds were being made. On the television screen, Louie gradually took his arms down from around his head and Dexter Beck jumped into the ring. Both were laughing and hugging each other.

"A total fuckin' knockout," Giambini finally said quietly. "I don't fuckin' believe it." He reached for a phone that wasn't there. "Hey, Rizzo...call Vegas for me, will ya? Make sure we ain't dreamin'." Rizzo started dialing.

"Hey, boss," said Lesko. "I thought this Fernandez was going blow the convention center or something after the fight. Nothing is happening."

Giambini looked at the television screen. "Leo, right now, I am *not* worried about that crazy Mexican. I got enough money to fight him and keep him from taking over my drug territory now. To hell with him!"

Rizzo closed his cell phone. "Boss, the boys in Vegas are just a little bit out of their heads right now. They said they have to scramble to get your cash, but they'll have it to you in a week."

Giambini spread his hands in a magnanimous gesture. "Hey...that's all I can ask, right?"

AS JACKIE TUCKED CYNTHIA into bed, the child looked up at Jackie and asked, "Jackie? Does this mean that the mean man will leave us alone now?"

Jackie lovingly ran her hand along Cynthia's head and said, "I sure hope so, Cindy-Windy. That's all we can ask, right?"

THE NEXT DAY, WEDNESDAY, all the news outlets in the city were talking about how Justice Security and Jim Dandy had saved thousands by disarming a bomb in the convention center, and that it had been placed by a man named Esteban Fernandez. They elaborated on the fact that Louie had been deliberately stretching the fight out to buy time to find the bomb and disarm it.

Louie had spoken with the boxing officials, and had the fight declared null and void. "I can't in good faith accept the Heavyweight belt knowing that I was prolonging the fight on purpose, regardless of the reason behind the delay," he said in a written statement.

Jacqueline Belew didn't think a thing about it when she heard about it.

Mickey Giambini didn't think a thing about it when he heard about it.

Leo Lesko and Vincent Lambosa didn't think a thing about it when they heard about it.

But the boys in Vegas thought about it when they heard about it. They thought about it a lot.

Chapter 5

A week later, Jackie put the kids on Mike Woods' bus for the trip to school. As each child got onto the bus, she hugged him or her, and kissed them on the cheek. Then, when Mike was ready to get on the bus, she hugged him, and kissed him...but not on the cheek.

Mike looked at her and said, "Jackie Blue, thank you for loving me."

Jackie smiled at the use of her nickname, and smiled back at the burly driver. "Right back atcha, mister!"

Mike smiled and said, "See you for dinner tonight, sugar. " He climbed on the bus and yelled out, "Who's ready for a trip on Mikey's Magic Bus?"

Shouts of "Me!" and "We are!" came from the seats, as Mike shut the doors and started the engine. They drove away, heading for school.

Jackie smiled as she watched the bus roll out of sight. It was amazing the difference that could be made in a week! She almost skipped up the sidewalk because she was so happy! She had a wonderful man in her life that she actually thought she might marry, and the children were happy with her and with Mike.

And Mickey Giambini had kept his word.

Jackie had not been bothered by anyone in the Giambini family ever since the boxing match. She supposed there were times when even the mob had enough money!

AROUND NOON, MICKEY Giambini was in his office. Rizzo had just come in with Giambini's lunch from the deli down the street.

Giambini wasn't moving. His hands rested on the desk. One hand was empty, and a cell phone was in the other. He was staring in front of him, at nothing, with his mouth slightly open.

"Boss?" said Rizzo. "You okay?"

Giambini didn't answer. He didn't seem to have heard Rizzo.

Rizzo set Giambini's lunch down on the corner of the desk and tried again, a little louder. "*Boss!*"

Giambini slowly looked at Rizzo. His eyes came back into focus, and, with an inarticulate cry, he slammed the cell phone down hard on the desk. He continued slamming the phone down, punctuating each slam with a four-letter swear word, until the phone shattered. He stood and threw the remains across the office with another inarticulate yell, then whirled to Rizzo. Giambini's face was a study of anger, with wide eyes and gritting teeth.

"Those sunzabitches in Vegas say we lost our bet, and they ain't sendin' us our money!" he shouted. "They say that since Washington had the fight declared fake, that made Pyle still the Champ, and the winner of the fight! So they say we lost all the money we bet on the fight!"

Rizzo looked shocked. "But...boss, he *won!* Washington *won the fuckin' fight!*"

"You *bet* he won the fuckin' fight! But, not according to those greedy bastards in Vegas!"

"Boss...that means...we got no money!"

Giambini's face went from deep anger, to confusion, to realization, and finally, to fear. He slumped down into opulent desk chair. "Oh, crap," he said quietly. "You're right, Rizzo. We got no money. Not enough, anyway." He put his head into his hands. "Oh, boy...what am I gonna do?"

Both men sat quietly for a moment, thinking.

"If that damn Vincent had never seen that Belew woman, we wouldn't be in this mess, boss."

Giambini slowly looked up. "Rizzo, that's *it!*"

"What's it, boss?"

"Get hold of Vincent, and tell him to bring me that Belew woman! Now!" Giambini began smiling. "I'll get my money back, one way or another!"

WHEN VINCENT'S CELL phone rang, he was active in very intense business negotiations with Steve, the owner of the convenience store near Jackie's house. They were negotiating in the beer cooler. Vincent made a sincere point with his right fist, and Steve conceded the point by falling to the floor to think about it for a moment. Vincent used the time-out to answer his phone.

"Lambosa," said Vincent into the phone.

"It's Rizzo. The boss wants your psychic lady friend in his office now. I repeat, *now.*"

"Understood." Vincent hung up the phone and put it back into his pocket, and reached down to pull Steve to his feet.

By the time Vincent left the store to pick up Jackie Belew, he was able to count Steve as a loyal paying customer.

JACKIE WAS SLICING tomatoes for a tossed salad to serve with dinner tonight. Her mind was drifting as she worked, thinking about Mike and the kids, and how she should probably begin the adoption process. Her case worker assured her that it would likely be only a formality.

"Hello again, puss," came a familiar voice from behind her.

Jackie jumped, looked up, then whirled to look behind her, paring knife in her hand.

Vincent knocked Jackie unconscious with a hard punch to her temple.

JACKIE SLOWLY REGAINED consciousness to the sound of men talking. She tried to move her head, but pain kept her from moving it quickly. She reached for the side of her head and felt a lump. The memory came rushing back. She jerked awake, eyes wide open.

She saw Mickey Giambini, Leo Lesko, Vincent, and Rizzo. Her stomach again turned to ice, and plummeted to somewhere below her feet.

Giambini said as he waved his finger between himself and her, "We gotta problem, you and me."

"Wha...why am I here? What problem?" she replied.

"Your little prediction last week about the boxing match. It went south."

"Huh? Went south? How? Washington won the fight!"

"Lemme explain, doll," said Giambini. And he did.

"How can they do that? He *won!*" said Jackie, terrified.

"Yeah, well, they did it," replied Giambini. "And now I got no money. I bet everything I had on that fight." He slammed his fist down on his desk. "*Everything!*" he shouted.

Jackie said nothing. She was afraid to say anything, which was good, because she couldn't think of a thing *to* say.

"So, you are gonna help me get it back," said Giambini, a touch of anger in his voice. "I got a room downstairs that's gonna turn into your home. You're gonna tell me the winners of every sport event I can come across, until I have the three hundred sixty million dollars that I would have won, *if you had given me the right fuckin' winner!*" He slammed his fist down again on his desk, punctuating each word.

Jackie flinched every time Giambini's fist hit the desk. "But...I can't stay here! I have children to take care of!"

Giambini looked at Jackie with steely, cold eyes. "Would you like for Vincent to go take care of the children?"

Jackie quickly shook her head. "No, sir," she said meekly.

"Then, Miss Belew," said Giambini, "I think you should go to your room, and get to work."

THE ROOM THAT RIZZO showed her was in the basement of the building. The door opened outward, and had three big night bolts that locked from the outside. She wouldn't be opening that door by herself.

Inside, there was a single bed...almost a cot. There was a sink, a toilet, and a small, stand-up shower. There was a small phone table, and a chair. The room was ten feet by ten feet.

"I'll be bringing your meals, and I'll bring a big bottle of water in a few minutes," said Rizzo. He fidgeted for a moment. "Miss, this wasn't my idea. I'm sorry about it. The boss should have avoided betting everything on one fight. But, when the boss gets an idea, he can't be talked out of it."

"Thank you, Mr. Rizzo," replied Jackie quietly. "We all do what we must."

Rizzo nodded. "Yes, ma'am, we do."

Rizzo left her alone. She heard the three bolts being thrown, and she knew she was in the deepest trouble she had ever been.

She hoped that the children would remember what she told them. If they didn't, she would *never* get out of here.

THE CHILDREN ARRIVED home at three-thirty, driven by the cheerful Mike Woods. They thought it was a bit odd that Jackie didn't come outside to greet them, but not out of the ordinary. It wasn't until they went inside and saw the sliced tomatoes and salad fixings on the counter. The paring knife was on the floor, looking sinister and out of place there.

Mike and the children went through the house thoroughly, calling Jackie's name, not expecting an answer. Mike secretly was expecting the worst, and was terrified that he would find Jackie dead in one of the beds upstairs, or stuffed into the freezer like poor Mrs. Morgan down the street.

But, his fears proved to be groundless. Jackie wasn't in the house.

Her purse, however...that was in the house, in her room. Exactly where it should have been.

The family finally came to the conclusion that Jackie had been kidnapped, probably by the Giambini mob.

"I THINK WE SHOULD DO what Jackie said to, but I think we should do it now," said Tommy.

"Why? Are you scared, Tommy?" asked Nicky, as if he was ready to pick on Tommy for being afraid.

"Stop it, Nicky," said Jennie Lou. "We're *all* afraid. We're afraid for us, and we're afraid for Jackie. So don't *even* act like you're not afraid!"

Mike, who in his heart agreed with Tommy, said, "I don't think so, Tommy. Jackie said to give it a couple of days, and we will. But, I hate waiting...I'm worried sick about her!"

Cynthia, who had been crying, climbed up into Mike's lap. "Do you think she'll be all right, Mike?" she asked meekly.

Mike summoned all of the bluster and good humor that he could, and said, "I think she'll be fine, cupcake...for a couple of days, anyway." To the other children, he said, "Okay, you got Big Mike watching you rats for a couple of days. Let's get this party started!"

Chapter 6

Justice Security, Incorporated owned its own building on a tree-lined street in a better part of the city. The six-story aboveground edifice occupied a large portion of a city block, with parking areas for visitors, and a landscaped, park-like green area on its south side. The building itself was constructed of three-foot-wide reinforced concrete walls. Each window was made of thick bulletproof glass, including the visitors' entrance door. The building extended six floors underground. The bottom three underground floors were used as a vehicle storage area, and housed various armor-plated and bullet resistant vehicles to be used as protective equipment for transporting and defending employees or clients. The next underground level was the armory. All types of weapons were stored in the climate-controlled armory, from revolvers and automatic pistols, to mortars, to surface-to-air missiles and launchers, and various armor-piercing weapons. Enough weaponry and ammunition were stored in the armory to take down a small country's government, should they be hired for such a thing...and they had done so, twice, a couple of years ago under an ultra-classified government contract. The floor above the armory was records storage. This floor contained the paper files, computers, data storage, and research areas needed for executing and completing client contracts. The final underground level was the garage for employee parking, and was accessed by a ground-level entrance contained by a thick, heavy steel door embedded into the concrete walls of the building.

At ground level, the first floor contained the reception area, the cafeteria, building security, and visitors' rest areas. The second and third floors were occupied by employee offices, conference rooms, smaller meeting rooms, and clerical services. The fourth floor housed executive offices and the situation room. The fifth floor was for guest housing, and the top floor contained residential apartments for the top level people of the company. The roof of the building had a helicopter pad, equipped with two armor-reinforced, stealth-equipped, black ops helicopters always ready to fly at a moment's notice.

The company also owned two private jets and two large cargo planes, which were housed at a private airfield just south of the city.

Justice Security had been formed a few years earlier by four college friends, who remained the directors and sole stockholders of the company.

Joey Justice, after whom the company was named, was a nondescript man. Standing at five feet ten inches, he had dark hair and intense brown eyes that usually missed nothing. He had founded the company with the premise of providing security services tempered with justice, as his name implied. He was very much in love with the lady in his life, who was also one of the cofounders of the company.

Misty Wilhite, the lady of Joey's life, stood five feet five. She had shoulder-length auburn hair, with green eyes. She was extremely attractive, but she had a punch that could drop a person twice her size. She, too, was very much in love with Joey, and shared his belief of security and justice. They had not married, because neither felt that it was necessary, although they had talked about it often.

Dexter Beck was the resident computer nerd. Standing one inch taller than Misty, Dexter was consistently underestimated by antagonists. Understanding usually followed, because Dexter also was a martial arts master, utilizing several methods of self-defense. The security and computer systems used by Justice Security were created, programmed, and maintained by Dexter.

Percival "King Louie" Washington was the fourth founding member of Justice Security. Louie stood four inches over six feet, and had a very imposing muscular build. He also was very intelligent and street-smart. His skin was the color of a milk chocolate bar, and he kept his head shaved. The other three founding members had nicknamed him "King Louie" in their first year of college because of his unfortunate facial resemblance to the cartoon character in the Jungle Book movie. It wasn't racial, and Louie knew it…just like if he had had a big nose, they would have nicknamed him "Baloo". Besides, anything was better than his given name of Percy.

These were the founding four partners. Justice Security had six partners, however – the founding four had invited two others to become full partner in the company.

Jessica Queen had originally been the executive secretary of the company, and had been offered a partnership a couple of years earlier, but had not felt she was ready to handle the responsibility that came with the job. She had reconsidered, and accepted the partnership recently. Jessica cared deeply for her friends and co-partners, and, despite her sometimes cutting sarcastic remarks, was often considered the heart and conscience of the company.

Megan Fisk had originally been Dexter's main computer security designer. She had recently taken charge of a group of field operatives, and performed her job exceptionally well while wounded, and had shown herself unusually adept at field work under fire. She and Dexter Beck had recently discovered that they were deeply in love with each other. Megan was offered a well-earned full partnership, and had eloped with Dexter following the experience at the convention center.

Each weekday morning at nine, the partners met in the situation room to discuss current and recurrent cases. If, for some reason, they couldn't be there in person, they would link into the meeting by a secure satellite feed. This was a requirement of the partners, because it kept everyone in the company informed of the status of the cases handled by each, should someone else have to step in to complete a case, or should a bailout or rescue become necessary. Today's meeting would have exceptions, since Dexter and Megan were on their honeymoon. They would not be expected to participate. Since their cases had taken them all over the world, into some fairly dangerous situations, bailouts and rescues sometimes were a necessity.

The company often contracted with the United States Government, and most of those contracts were top secret. Domestic contracts were overseen by a government liason, an agent assigned to the local FBI office. His name was Marcus Moore. Overseas contracts for the government were usually assigned to them by high-level members of the White House, and overseen and assisted by whatever CIA agents might be in an area in which the security firm was operating.

Justice Security did not limit itself to government contracts, however. Making a profit on government cases was sometimes difficult, so the company often provided its services to private concerns and individuals. Joey reminded his partners, and the people that worked for him, that clients of the company did not bring small cases to them. Every case represented people, and those people needed help, not dismissal...no matter what the potential profit. Those that could pay, did...those that couldn't were treated no differently. Joey once took a case for a twelve-year-old boy who was being bullied at school, and assigned a five-member team to take care of it...the company's payment was some astounding artwork by the boy, along with a couple of polished rocks from the boy's collection. Joey kept the sketches, which were framed and hung on the walls of his office, and Misty kept the polished rocks and had them made into necklaces.

On this particular Friday morning, Misty Wilhite was at the front desk in the Justice Security lobby. Misty was the partner in charge of the "grunts", as they were affectionately called – the uniformed security personnel of the company. Second in charge of the "grunts" was Tony Armstrong, the guard that saw to the operation of the lobby and reception areas as well. Misty and Tony had just gone over the basic overnight "grunt" reports, and were discussing what people were needed, and where, for the next couple of days.

"Misty," said Tony, "how's Turk doing with the executive secretary position?"

Misty smiled. Tony and Turk were long-time friends, and had actually came to the company together. Turk Wendall, a huge man even more imposing than Louie Washington, had taken over the executive secretary position at Justice Security after the untimely and violent death of Patti Hoehn at the hands of Esteban Fernandez. Turk had shown an unusual proficiency for the job, and had accepted it on a permanent basis.

"He's doing fine, Tony," replied Misty. "I think he could scare monsters away with that look of his."

Tony grunted. "Hmph. The only monster around here *is* Turk."

While Misty was giggling at Tony's remark, Tony's attention was drawn to the glass double doors that opened into the lobby. He saw a group of five children with crutches, leg braces, and wheelchairs entering the building, followed by a good-sized man. The man appeared to be in charge of the group.

Misty noticed the group as well. She quickly ran through the appointment book in her hands. She didn't find any school tours listed there. She wondered what these children wanted?

The group made their way to the reception desk. Tony greeted them.

"Hi, kids! Hello, sir. Welcome to Justice Security. I'm Tony Armstrong. May I help you?"

The young woman in the wheelchair took the lead. "We'd like to see Joey Justice, please."

Tony smiled. "Do you have an appointment, Miss?"

The young lady's face fell, and gradually so did the others in the group. "No, sir, we don't. Is an appointment required?"

"Not always, Miss. It depends on the situation. Now, in a general way, what's the problem?"

The kids all looked around at each other, then at the man standing behind them.

Tony, understanding their hesitance, said, "I don't want specifics. Just generalities. It helps me determine whether the urgency of your case is strong enough that I need to break into Mr. Justice's day for you. If he's busy, he may ask you to make an appointment. If it's urgent, he can reschedule what he has planned so that he can see you." Tony shrugged and held up his hands. "So, what's up? What can we do for you?"

The young woman in the wheelchair looked at the man, who shrugged and nodded.

"Our foster mom is missing, and hasn't been home since sometime Wednesday. We think she's been kidnapped," said the girl in the wheelchair.

"I see," said Tony, nodding. He looked at Misty, who had been listening. She nodded, and took over.

"Hi, guys," said Misty. "My name is Misty Wilhite, and I'm going to see that you talk to Mr. Justice. How's that?"

The group all smiled with relief, immediately forming a liking for Misty.

"Okay, so what are your names?" asked Misty.

For the first time, the man spoke. "My name is Mike Woods. I'm the bus driver for these kids, and Jackie and I are...well..."

"They're in *looove*," said Nicky.

Mike blushed, and said, "Well, that's true, I guess. These kids are," he pointed at each as he introduced them, "Jennie Lou Gwin, Phillip Wheeler, Nicky Watson, Tommy Larkin, and Cynthia Rudisill." He looked at Misty, naked hurt in his eyes. "We got a story to tell you, Miss Wilhite...and parts of it my be kinda hard to believe." He leaned closer to her, and whispered, "It involves the Giambini crime family."

Misty raised her eyebrows. She was surprised. The partners had often discussed how odd it was that they had not had run-ins with the Giambinis. Now, it apparently was being dropped into their laps. Marcus Moore, their FBI liason, would have a field day with it.

"In that case, Mr. Woods," she said, "please get your bus, and park it in our private garage in the basement. Tony will direct you. I'll take the children to Mr. Justice's office. We have a brief meeting at nine this morning, but it will be short. Then Mr. Justice will join you and the children in his office."

Mike nodded. "Thank you, Miss Wilhite."

Misty turned to the children. "Okay, kids, follow me!"

Misty led the way to the elevator, and got all of the children on board. The elevator opened at the fourth floor, and the children all piled out, then froze. A huge, muscular, black man was standing beside the desk, staring at them with a fierce look. When he saw Misty, he raised his eyebrows in an unspoken question.

"Okay, kids, this is Turk Wendall. He's a good man, and will put you in Mr. Justice's office while I go to the meeting." Misty looked at Turk. "Clients, Turk. I'll let them tell you what's up, while I go to the meeting. A man is with them – his name is Mike Woods. Tony's helping him park in the garage, and he'll be up in a bit to join them. Please let the children wait in Joey's office, would you?"

"Glad to," replied Turk. He turned his glare back on, and directed it at the children. "And nobody's gonna touch nothin', right?"

The children all shook their heads.

AT THE END OF THE MEETING, Joey was walking back to his office when Turk stopped him.

"You got people in your office, boss."

Joey stopped. "Really? Who?"

"Kids."

Joey smiled. "Well, what do these kids want, Turk?"

"They want to hire you."

"Why do they want to hire me?"

Turk fidgeted in his chair. "I'd rather they tell you, boss...if you don't mind."

Joey, looking puzzled, nodded. "Okay, Turk. I'll talk to them." He crossed to his office and entered it.

Misty peeked around the corner from the hall.

"Did he go for it?" asked Misty.

"He's talkin' to them, Misty," replied Turk.

Inside the office were five children, three boys and two girls. They ranged in age from about ten to about sixteen or seventeen. One of the girls and two of the boys wore leg braces, and the girl had crutches strapped to her arms, and it was obvious that she had cerebral palsy. The other girl was in a wheelchair, and the oldest boy was sitting on the couch beside her, rocking back and forth rapidly. Joey guessed that the boy was autistic, and the girl appeared to be a quadriplegic.

"Hi, guys. I'm Joey Justice. What can I do for you?" said Joey, as he crossed to sit down in one of the soft chairs.

The girl in the wheelchair faced him. "Mr. Justice, we live in a group home under the care of our foster mom, Jacqueline Belew. She hasn't come home for the past two nights. We're very scared for her...and for us. We'd like to hire you to find her."

The autistic boy, punctuating his words with his rocking, said forcefully, "Find Jackie *Blue!* Find Jackie *Blue!* Find Jackie *Blue!*"

The door to Joey's office opened, and a man walked in, and over to Joey, with his right hand out to shake. "Mr. Justice, my name is Mike Woods. I guess I'm kind of in charge of these rats right now. Let me introduce you to them, and then we'll tell you our story."

JOEY LEANED BACK IN his chair. "Wow," he said quietly.

Inside, Joey was seething. From what these kids had said, it appeared that Mickey Giambini had provided the explosives that had been planted at the convention center. If that was the case, Joey wanted a crack at Giambini. He wanted it bad. But, it wasn't a decision that he felt he could make on his own...or one he could make in anger.

"Excuse me just for a moment, would you?" Joey said to his guests. He leaned forward to the outer office buzzer. "Hey, Turk?"

"Yep."

Joey shook his head, smiling at the big man. "Would you please get in touch with Louie and Jessica, and ask them to come to my office ASAP? And tell Misty to stop lingering out there and come inside."

"Yes, boss."

Nicky nudged Tommy with widened eyes. Joey noticed.

The door to Joey's office opened, and Misty joined them.

Joey looked up at Misty with a smile playing around his lips. "Intended therapy, sweet love?"

Misty smiled back. "It sounded like a simple case...something to get your mind off of Fernandez."

Joey snickered and turned to his guests. "Have you all had breakfast? We have a fully staffed cafeteria in the building. It serves what you want when you want it."

The kids all looked at each other, hesitant to ask.

Joey smiled. "They'll even deliver up here, if you'd prefer," he told them.

Mike broke the silence. "I'd sure like a good, strong cup of coffee, Mr. Justice...and maybe a doughnut or something."

That did it for the kids. They all started talking at once. Joey raised his hands in a "stop" gesture, laughing. "Wait a minute, guys!" He pressed the buzzer again. "Hey, Turk!"

"Yep."

"Can you come in here with a pen and pad, please?"

"Yep."

A few seconds later, Turk lumbered through the door with a pencil and a steno pad.

"Turk, my man!" said Joey. "Would you be kind enough to take breakfast orders all around, and ask the cafeteria to deliver them here?"

"Sure, boss." Turk opened his pad, then turned to Jennie Lou first.

After everyone's order had been taken, Turk said, "Louie will be here in ten minutes. Jessica should be here in fifteen."

Joey nodded. "Thanks, big buddy." Turk left the room.

A FEW MINUTES LATER, a knock sounded on Joey's office door, then it opened. Percival "King Louie" Washington stepped in.

Joey, who had been showing off the sketches made by the twelve-year-old boy, smiled and said, "Louie! Thanks for coming!"

"Glad to do it, Joey," replied Louie. "I was kinda bored, just lookin' over a possible job. What's up?"

The children were all looking at Louie with wide eyes. Joey smiled at this.

"Louie, I'd like to introduce you to some boxing fans," said Joey. Louie raised his eyebrows, surprised. Joey put his hand on each child's shoulder as he introduced them, and Louie nodded at each name. "This is Phillip Wheeler. Jennie Lou Gwin. Cynthia Rudisill. Tommy Larkin. And this young man is Nicky Watson...he's probably your biggest fan."

Louie held out his hand to Nicky. Nicky couldn't speak, but put his hand in Louie's.

"Good to meet you folks," said Louie. He shook hands with each of the younger children, and with Phillip. With Jennie Lou, he knelt in front of her chair, and took her hand in his. "Young lady, the pleasure is all mine." Then he kissed her hand and placed it back in its comfortable position. Jennie Lou smiled and blushed.

"And this gentleman," said Joey, "is Mike Woods. He's temporarily in charge of these young people."

"It's a real pleasure to meet you, Mr. Washington," said Mike as he shook Louie's hand.

"Hey, man, call me Louie. That goes for you kids, too."

"Louie, we're waiting for Jessica before we get started," said Joey.

"Then we should get started, don't you think?" said Jessica as she breezed through the door. "I've been here simply for*ever*!" She smiled at each child as she shook their hands and introductions were made.

Breakfast arrived, and each guest was served. The Justice Security partners noted with approval that Phillip and Cynthia took turns assisting Jennie Lou. They also noted that Mike Woods kept a close eye on all of the children, ready to do anything he needed to for them.

Joey set down a coffee mug he had been holding, and said, "Jennie Lou, would you and your family please repeat what you told me so that Misty, Louie, and Jessica can hear?"

Jennie Lou swallowed a bite of bacon and said, "Everything, Mr. Justice?"

"It's Joey, sweetheart. And, yes, please...everything."

Jennie Lou took a deep breath, asked Cynthia for a sip of juice, and told the group the events of the past few days from beginning to end, with assistance from the other children, and from Mike Woods. When she got to the part about the convention center, Louie spoke.

"That dirty motherfuh...um, I mean 'that snake'!" said Louie, catching himself.

Cynthia and Nicky both giggled. The other children grinned, and even Mike Woods smiled.

Jennie Lou finished her story.

Joey turned to his friends. "So, we have an opportunity to not only help these folks by finding Miss Belew and bringing her home, but to do some work on the most powerful crime family in the city for assisting Fernandez in trying to kill us. I want to take the case, but I couldn't in good conscience take the case without a consensus from the partners. Since Dexter and Megan are still gone until Monday, that leaves the four of us to decide, and it would have to be unanimous. It's going to be dangerous, but I think we can handle it. We could bloody his nose a little bit. Take a few minutes and think about it, then let's discuss your ideas."

"I don't need no few minutes to think about nuthin'," said Louie. "Let's go get that sorry..." He looked around at the children. "Let's see what we can do," he finished.

"I heard a partial account downstairs," said Misty. "Since I brought the children up and put them in your office, I think you know what my vote is. Let's get him."

Jessica had been watching everyone's faces. She knew what her partners wanted, but she also knew that Giambini wasn't the only story in the room. "I think we need to focus on getting Miss Belew back to her family first," she said. "We also need to find a way to get the Giambinis to leave her alone once we do. After that, if you want to go after him, I'm all for it." She leaned forward in her chair. "If the focus is Miss Belew and her family, I vote yes. If it's only to 'get Giambini', I will vote no. Which is it, partners?"

Misty smiled at Jessica. Jessica was relieved that Misty got it. Both Joey and Louie looked a little ashamed, but rebounded.

"Of course, the priority is getting Miss Belew back and ensuring that this family isn't bothered any more," said Joey.

"Yeah," said Louie. "But nothin' says we can't be...aggressive...with our ensuring." Then he smiled.

Jessica nodded. "Agreed. Let's do it."

Joey turned to the group. "We'll get Miss Belew back for you, kids. In the meantime, I strongly recommend that you all, including Mr. Woods, become guests of Justice Security, for safety's sake. We have plenty of guest quarters on the fifth floor, with everything that any of you might need."

"We even have a first-aid station in the building, with a fully licensed psychiatrist on staff," added Misty. "We also have access to FBI medical facilities if needed. Sometimes it helps to contract with the government."

"You mean we can stay *here?*" asked Nicky, wide-eyed.

"With *Louie?*" asked Tommy, similarly wide-eyed.

"Can he teach us how to box?" asked Nicky.

"And can he show us how to build our muscles, so we'll be strong?" asked Tommy.

Phillip, who had been quietly rocking behind Jennie Lou's wheelchair, blurted, "*Louie!*"

Louie, surprised by the outbursts from the boys, said, "Now, wait a minute! I ain't no babysitter!" When he saw the boys' faces fall, he added, "But I sure 'nuff can find some time to show some boys a few things in the weight room and the gym." He looked at Cynthia and Jennie Lou. "And that goes for some *girls,* too. Ya'll ain't gettin' outta nuthin' just 'cause you girls. Look at Misty here – she could kick me in the face 'fore I knew what happened. And it would *hurt,* too!"

Jennie Lou said quietly, "I don't think I'll be kicking anyone, sir."

Louie squatted beside her. "Maybe not, sugarplum...but we gonna trip out this wheelchair with some *stuff.* We got a lab for things just like that. You wait and see." He leaned forward and kissed her forehead.

"Mr. Woods," said Joey.

"It's Mike, please, Joey."

Joey nodded acknowledgement. "I know you drive a bus for the children, but can you take a few days off?"

Mike nodded. "Yeah. Right now, these guys are my only clients. I get referrals from the school system when new kids come into the system, but, for now, this is it."

"Good. You need to be here, too...both for the kids and for your own safety. The kids will skip school today, mainly because I don't have enough time to arrange everything I need to arrange. First things first, however. I will need you to go to the kids' home and pack clothes and necessities for them, like medicines or anything else that relates to their condition. Either Misty or Jessica will accompany you, along with a couple of grunts." He looked at Jennie Lou. "Would you please go with him? To help him get everything you all need?"

Jennie Lou smiled and nodded.

Mike looked puzzled. "Grunts?"

Joey smiled. "Sorry. It's an in-house term for uniformed security." He turned to the children to include them. "Until this case is resolved, none of you will leave this building without two grunts at your side. Period. If we can't keep you alive, what will Miss Jackie have to come home to once we find her?" The kids all looked solemn. "All of you need to realize that this is deadly serious business. The Giambini mob is very dangerous, and won't hesitate to kill any of you if they think it will advance whatever their business happens to be. They're not as bad as, say, Esteban Fernandez, but they're bad enough. We have to take precautions, and stick to them."

Jessica said, "I'll take the group to their home. I'd like to get to know Mike and Jennie Lou better."

Joey nodded. "Great, Jess. Would you and Misty please show everyone where their quarters are? That way, they can see what we have, and figure out what they need from home."

"Sure. Come on, guys."

Louie stood, too. "I think I'll tag along, and take the kids down to the gym. No time like now to get started on the physical stuff, right, guys?"

Shouts of "Yeah!" and "All *right!*" echoed through Joey's office.

"Are you okay with this?" Misty whispered to Joey.

"Of course," Joey whispered back. "I have a couple of phone calls to make, but I think we can get started today."

Misty smiled. "That's my man."

Joey kissed her. "I love you, sweet lady."

"Right back atcha."

Mike Woods eased over to Joey. "Joey, I don't want to beat around the bush, and I don't want to seem rude, but I don't know how we're going to pay for all of this. We're not the richest people in the world."

"Not a problem, Mike. It's covered."

"Really?"

Joey nodded. "It's covered. Trust me on this one. Our world doesn't revolve around money." He pointed to the children and whispered, "Don't you think that their safety is more important than any money?"

Mike nodded once, sharply. "You bet your ass it is."

"We agree. That's why it's covered. Now go get that stuff! We gotta get you guys buttoned up inside here!"

The group filed out of Joey's office, all going to the fifth floor to see the facilities. Joey stayed behind and turned to the telephone.

Chapter 7

Joey's first call was to the state's governor to arrange for temporary joint custody of the children, shared equally with Jacqueline Belew. To the governor, Joey explained the full story of what had happened, since the governor knew how to keep secrets. The governor agreed to push the Department of Children's Services Commissioner, a political appointee, to ensure that Justice Security had full temporary joint custody. He told Joey that the papers for the children would be inside the Justice Security building within an hour. Joey thanked the governor and hung up.

Joey's second call was to Marcus Moore, an FBI agent that acted as domestic liason for Justice Security.

"Marcus Moore."

"Hi, Marcus. This is Joey."

"Hey, City Savior! What's cooking?"

"Marcus, we just had a hot one dumped into our laps. I could sure use your help with this one."

"Wow...Joey, how much help do you need? I'm a little out of pocket right now. I'm working a hot case with Nicholas Turner, but we can postpone it if we have to."

Joey, knowing that Nicholas Turner and Marcus Moore were best friends, didn't want to pull Marcus away from what may be a big case for Turner. So, he said, "Well, the case involves Mickey Giambini, Marcus. But...if you can direct me to someone in the Bureau that could answer questions about him, I'd really be grateful...and you could keep helping Turner."

Marcus whistled. "Damn, Joey!" Then, Joey heard Marcus say to someone else, "Oops...sorry, punkin." Then to Joey, "Man, do you have a death wish or something? First, you piss off Esteban Fernandez...now you're going after Mickey Giambini? You've got great big, hairy, brass *cojones*, I'll say that! Okay, the guy you want to talk to is Johnny Yates. He's our city's resident FBI guy for mob activity. He can probably tell you anything you need to know. I can call him for you if you'd like."

"Would you, Marcus? And would you please ask him to come to the fourth floor at two this afternoon? And the big one, buddy: can we trust him?"

Joey could hear the smile in Marcus's voice. "You can trust him like you trust me, Joey...and I'll tell him the same thing about you. Hey, wait a minute, Joey." Joey could hear that Marcus covered the phone, and he could hear voices. One of the voices sounded like a child, but Joey couldn't be sure. Then, Marcus was back. "Joey, if you need us – and I mean Nicky and I – you just call and we'll come running to bail your sorry butt out. Okay?"

Joey smiled. "I'll definitely keep that in mind, Marcus. Thanks!" Joey tried to say, "And good luck!" but Marcus had already disconnected.

Joey then called Doctor Caleb Mitchell, the in-house psychiatrist, and explained about the children, and asked him to try to check them out.

"Joey, I'm not big on general medicine. You know that."

"I know, Caleb. I just want to make sure that the kids are healthy, and what we can and can't do. I mean, if I leave Louie alone, he'll have them all doing jumping jacks and bench presses."

Caleb laughed. "I'll hold him back, Joey. But I really don't think you have to worry about Louie. If anyone loves kids more than you do, it's Louie. I'll call you after I check them out."

Joey put his phone back on the hook. He looked down at his desk for a moment, lost in thought, wondering if this might have been a job for Nicholas Turner instead of Justice Security...

Nahhh...

JESSICA LED THE WAY for the group. When the elevator stopped on the fifth floor, they all piled out. Louie tagged along behind the main group. Eventually, all three boys drifted back so that they were walking with him.

Pied piper, thought Misty to herself, and smiled. Then, she noticed that both girls were keeping pace with her. *Uh-oh...me too, I guess.*

Jessica walked to the end of the hall, her long, brown pony-tailed hair swinging back and forth with each step. She stopped in front of one of the apartments and turned to her followers.

"Okay, kids, each apartment is set up a little like Embassy Suites," Jessica told them. "Each one has living room, kitchenette, bathroom, and either one or two bedrooms, plus *lots* of closet space. By kitchenette, I mean it has a full-sized stove, refrigerator, dishwasher, and sinks, but they aren't enclosed into a room by themselves...they actually are part of the living room. Most folks that stay for an extended stay don't use the kitchenette because we have a fully staffed, twenty-four hour cafeteria downstairs...and they deliver. But, the kitchenette is there if you choose to use it." She started to turn toward the apartment door, stopped, and turned back to the kids. "I don't expect any of you children to use the kitchen. Mr. Woods is free to use one if he wishes." Jessica smiled and turned to the door again, opening it.

The room inside was a young man's dream. It had a dark leather sofa and a couple of chairs to match. There was a huge high – definition television mounted on the wall opposite form the sofa, and on a small table underneath were three different video game systems, a blu-ray DVD player, and a surround sound base unit.

"This is where you three boys will stay," said Jessica. "There are two bedrooms, each with bunk beds. Phillip, I'm sorry about that...but you'll have a room to yourself, and you won't have to worry about choosing top or bottom bunk. They're both yours."

Tommy stammered, "How...how big is..."

Jessica smiled as she answered what she anticipated was Tommy's question. "The television is seventy-five inches, diagonally measured. Will that be large enough, boys?"

Tommy and Nicky both excitedly nodded their approval.

"Phillip," said Jessica, "will you be okay here with the boys?"

Phillip began rocking back and forth on his feet, smiling.

"He'll be fine, Miss Jessica," said Jennie Lou.

Jessica nodded once, and said, "Okay, then. Let's check out the girls' room, shall we?"

The group all followed Jessica down the hall. She stopped at the second door to the right of the boys' room. She grasped the knob and said, "Your rooms are almost identical to the boys' rooms, with one exception: There is a regular bed in one of the rooms for Jennie Lou. Cindy, someone will always be available to help you with Jennie Lou, or anything else you might need. I'll even give you my room phone number – I live on this floor, and can be here in a jiffy if you need anything."

"Thank you, Miss Jessica," said Cynthia.

Jennie Lou smiled at Jessica, who smiled back.

"Okay, if everyone will follow me again, I'll show Mr. Woods to his room."

"My name is Mike, Miss Jessica."

"And mine is Jessica, Mike. Please drop the 'Miss'. That goes for all of you!" She glared around at the children as if she were angry.

"Does that go for me, too, Miss Jessica?" asked Louie.

"No, you big sack of fertilizer...you have to call me 'O Wonderous Madam'." The children all laughed. Louie smiled.

Jessica led the group back to the left, to the door that they had passed by. She opened the door to show a room similar to the ones occupied by the children, but more grown up. Mike nodded his satisfaction.

"Thank you folks for this," said Mike.

Jessica looked at Mike. "It's what we do, Mike."

"We protect our clients," added Misty.

"Damn right," said Louie.

"Now, I need Mike, Phillip, and Jennie Lou," said Jessica. "It's time to go get your clothes and things."

Jackie had been dozing. She had no idea whether it was night or day, or even what time it was. When the sound of the locks opening penetrated her nap, she awoke immediately, and sat up on her cot.

She had not been cooperating. She had decided that if the kids had done what she told them to do and had gone to Justice Security, there was nothing Mickey Giambini could do to her that would make her cooperate. There had been quiet threats, and Jackie didn't give any predictions. There had been shouted threats with the same effect. There had been implied threats. Still, Jackie would not give them any predictions.

Jackie's captors had begun withholding food several hours ago, and Jackie's stomach was growling...but she still told them nothing. So far, there had been no physical abuse, and no one had withheld water. She wondered how long that would last.

Rizzo came through the door carrying a tray. The tray had a salad, what looked like a burger, and a slice of pie, with a bottle of iced tea. He placed it on the table, and turned to Jackie.

"Miss Belew, you know I'm against keeping you here, right?" he asked.

Jackie nodded.

He gestured to the tray on the small table. "Then don't let that fool you. They'll be in later to try stronger tactics. Be prepared."

"Thank you, Mr. Rizzo," said Jackie quietly.

"I just wish I could do something," he said. Then he turned around and left.

But he made sure the locks were engaged.

Jackie knew that Rizzo wouldn't help her. He valued his life a little too much. But she did appreciate the sympathy.

When she looked down at her tray, the salad and half the burger were gone already. Jackie was so hungry, she didn't even remember eating them. She quickly finished her meal.

A few minutes after eating, she heard the door locks disengaging once more. Vincent entered the room, followed by Mickey Giambini. Giambini closed the door, then folded his hands in front of him, looking down at Jackie.

Finally, he spoke.

"Miss Belew," he said.

Jackie looked up at him.

"We've tried everything we can think of to...entice...you into giving us what we ask. Now it's time for, say," he spread his hands wide, "*sterner* measures."

Jackie said nothing.

Giambini, in a fit of anger, backhanded Jackie on the side of the face. Jackie almost fell from the chair. Tears came to her eyes, as much from the humiliation as the pain. She kept her head turned as she fought down the crying jag that wanted to bubble to the surface.

Vincent took out a horse racing form and slammed it down on the table in front of her.

"Give me some winners, puss," said Vincent.

Jackie shook her head.

"Last chance, puss," Vincent said. "Give me some winners."

"No," she replied.

Giambini shook his head sadly. "Then, Miss Belew, you leave me no choice." He turned to Vincent. "Go to Miss Belew's house and kill one of the kids. I don't care which one. Maybe that will convince her."

The two men left the room, and secured the door locks.

Jackie's stomach fell to the floor. She felt fairly certain that the children had done what she asked, but what if they hadn't?

Oh, dear God...*what if they hadn't?*

THE ONLY VEHICLE IN the Justice Security garage that could accommodate everyone was not set up for wheelchair access. Mike Woods suggested that the group make the trip in his school bus, which was wheelchair accessible, but Jessica insisted on a Justice Security vehicle, because they were heavily armored, and the windows were bulletproof. Jennie Lou was still able to accompany the group, thanks to Phillip and Louie.

Once Louie saw that his strength could be used on the trip for carrying either Jennie Lou or her wheelchair, he decided to tag along on the journey. Joey also came downstairs to the garage, and announced that he was going, too.

"I feel like I need to go. It might give me some insights into Jackie that might help in finding her," he told the others.

Misty said that she would stay with the three younger children, and help get them settled.

Joey looked at all three of the children and said, "If you play video games with her, be careful." He pointed to her. "*She's* the reason the video games are installed in those two guest rooms. She'll mop the floor with you guys." He held up his hands in surrender when Misty looked at him with wide open eyes. "I'm just sayin'..."

"Hmph," said Misty, and kissed Joey. "Be careful, main man. I love you."

Joey gave Misty a big hug as the children watched. "And I love you, lady." To the kids he said, "Be careful, guys...I'm just sayin'...," he repeated.

Louie said, from inside the armored bus, "Will you two please knock it off? You as bad as Dex and Megan!"

Jessica said, "Joey, if the FBI man will be here at two, we'd better get going."

Two "grunts" had been assigned to drive the bus and add to the security. Driving would be done by Patty Ferguson, an attractive, blonde, petite woman. Brandon King, a young, athletic, coffee-and-cream-skinned man, would be riding shotgun. Both were relatively new to Justice Security, but had been highly recommended by both Tony Armstrong and by Misty.

As Joey followed Jessica onto the bus, he noticed that Patty was already in the driver's seat, searching maps and the GPS for routes to the children's house that would be both fast and safe, and that Brandon was standing beside the open door, looking around the garage with quick glances that took in everything in his line of sight. He stopped beside Brandon and said, "Mr. King, do you really think that you need to be so vigilant in our own house?"

Brandon turned to Joey and said, "With all due respect, sir, we have clients with us that are in danger. You have a price on your head big enough to persuade possible turncoats within our organization. I speak for Patty as well as myself when I say we will keep watching as long as either you or clients are our responsibility, and we will take appropriate action to keep either or both safe. But, to answer your question, sir, yes. Until Esteban Fernandez drops that price on your head, I *will* be vigilant in our own house." He began scanning the garage again.

Joey, taken aback by Brandon's comments, more by the truth in them than the fact that Brandon had the guts to say them, said, "I apologize, Brandon. You are very right." He climbed onto the bus and sat down, deep in thought. He had not thought of the possibility of a traitor in the organization.

The thought intrigued him.

It also frightened him.

Chapter 8

The two-toned brown van from Justice Security parked at the curb in front of and a few yards down from Jackie's house.

Brandon exited first, scanning the area, right hand on his sidearm. He looked inside, caught Patty's eye, and nodded.

"Looks safe, sir," she said to Joey. "I'll be bringing up the rear."

"Man, I feel safer already," said Louie. He stood up, unbuckled Jennie Lou, and picked her up. "You know, I'm really glad these two are watchin' out, 'cause it ain't like I got any experience doin' this or nuthin'."

As Louie passed Brandon, the younger man said, "Just taking care of my elders, sir."

Louie stopped and looked at Brandon. "Man, you lucky my arms is full of girl right now." Both men held their stone faces for another minute, then both burst out laughing.

"You all right, kid," said Louie. "Come see me later. I need a replacement for Turk." Phillip had brought out Jennie Lou's wheelchair, and Louie set her down in it. "Ever since folks figured out that Turk is fahn sec-ree-tarial material. Prob'ly just wants to chase his big ass around the desk."

"I chase him around the desk every day," said Jessica, climbing down the bus steps. "Sometimes Turk lets me catch him, too."

"Just proves one thang," replied Louie. "My man Turk got no taste."

Joey came down the steps, followed by Mike Woods and Patty. Patty secured the door to the bus.

"Lead on, Jessica. Let's get this done," said Joey.

As the group reached the front porch, Brandon and Patty stood on each side of the front door. Mike Woods unlocked the door and opened it. Brandon entered and slid to the right. Patty entered and slid to the left. Both had weapons drawn, pointed to the floor.

The front door opened into a hall that ran through the house from the front to the back. On the right, and a couple of feet down the hall, was the door to the living room. A few feet down from the living room door, still on the right, was the staircase that led to the second floor. Past the stairs was the door to Jackie's bedroom, and, under the stairs, was the door to the basement. On the left, and a couple of feet down the hall, was the door to the dining room and kitchen. This was a combination room that stretched the length of the house from front to back. In the kitchen, the back door opened into a walled-off area that Jackie and the kids referred to as the "coat room". It was open on both ends, and the walls were not as tall as the kitchen ceiling. It had a ceiling of its own, and the space between its ceiling and the kitchen ceiling was used as storage. One end exited into the kitchen, and the other end exited into the hall, across from Jackie's bedroom. Inside the "coat room" was the entrance to a narrow stairwell also leading to the second floor, often referred in other houses as "the servants' stairs". In Jackie's house, they were simply "the back stairs". A bathroom was located inside the dining room/kitchen. The second story had four small bedrooms and two small bathrooms squeezed into its space, and the third floor housed an attic that was used for storage.

As Brandon and Patty worked their way down the hall, the group stepped into the hall and closed the front door behind them. Joey and Louie shared a glance and a smile at the youthful enthusiasm. Both men were remembering younger days in which they were as careful as the two younger team members. Experience had taught them that they didn't always have to be *quite* so vigilant...especially in the suburbs.

VINCENT PONDERED WHICH kid to kill as he drove to Jackie's neighborhood. He wanted a challenge, and the only one that might provide that would be the big kid that he almost shot a few days ago.

That kid almost scared Vincent.

"ALL CLEAR," SAID PATTY, coming down the stairs.

"Okay, then," said Jessica. "Time for clothes. Jennie Lou, I assume your bedroom is upstairs?"

"Yes, ma'am," Jennie Lou replied.

"Oh, my gosh," Jessica said. "Today, I am a 'ma'am.'"

Louie started laughing. "Dat mean you gettin' old, Jess."

"I'm the same age as you, Percival."

Louie stopped laughing and looked around wide-eyed. "She sho' don't look twenty-one, does she?"

Everyone laughed.

"Phillip, will you and the twenty-one-year-old please take Jennie Lou upstairs?" asked Jessica. "Mike, would you and Joey please go to Miss Jackie's bedroom and throw together a few things? Jennie Lou and I will inspect what you pick out when we come downstairs."

"Aye, aye, captain," said Joey, throwing a mock salute.

As Louie, Phillip, Jennie Lou, and Jessica went upstairs, Joey motioned Brandon and Patty over.

"Brandon, " said Joey. "Watch the front door. Sing out if you see anything."

"Yes, sir," replied Brandon.

"Miss Ferguson, you're with Mike and I. You're helping us choose Jackie's things."

Patty smirked.

"I don't know about anybody else, but I'm not giving Jessica a chance to make fun of us if I can help it," said Joey with a smile.

FIFTEEN MINUTES LATER, everyone was gathering in the foyer. Jessica, with Jennie Lou's help, had approved the choices made for Jackie's bag.

"Not bad, guys," she said suspiciously, moving her eyes between Joey, Mike, and Patty. Joey and Mike both tried to look innocent, while Patty remained expressionless.

Jessica turned to Phillip and said, "Phillip, would you please go upstairs and get those last two suitcases?"

Phillip turned and went up the stairs.

WHEN JACKIE FOUND VINCENT sitting at the kitchen table the first time, Vincent had picked the lock and entered through the back door, which opened into the coat room. He chose this method of entry again.

As he eased the back door open, Vincent could hear voices coming from his left, just beyond the back stairs, originating in the hall. He closed the back door, careful to make no noise, drew his shiny stainless steel semiautomatic pistol, and tiptoed to the hall entrance. He slowly eased an eye around the door facing, trying to see who was talking.

The first things that caught his eye were the two-toned brown uniforms. *Hmph...not cops. Justice Security!* he thought to himself. *A black dude and a puss. Then another older puss...crip in the wheelchair...big bus driver...Holy shit! Is that Joey Justice? It IS! The big man himself! And beside him, with his big black hands on the crip's wheelchair handles! It's Louie Washington! Louie Washington...the sonuvabitch that caused this whole problem! I have hit the jackpot!*

As Vincent ever so slowly raised his pistol with his right hand braced against the door facing, back to the coat room, his mind was racing. *Which one? Which? Mickey told me to kill one of the kids, but if I killed Washington, he'd be just as happy. I'll only get one shot. Then I'll have to run for it.* His aim wavered between Louie and Jennie Lou as his mind raced. *Which one? The crip...or Washington...I think I better kill*

Vincent's thoughts abruptly stopped as stars burst in his head and his body slammed across the hall into Jackie's bedroom door. His gun clattered halfway up the hall as he collapsed briefly onto the floor.

MIKE WOODS THOUGHT that he had never seen five people move as quickly as the people from Justice Security. From the first noise, five guns had been drawn and aimed down the hall before Mike registered that there *was* a noise. Then, Mike did what his instinct told him to...he blocked Jennie Lou from whatever was down the hall.

PHILLIP HAD AUTISM, but his IQ was extremely high. His mind raced like wildfire, often processing several different things at once, and the subjects would astound a normal person. His autism often prevented him from expressing his ideas and thought processes, and sometimes prevented him from communicating at all. He was there, in the moment, but was usually unable to participate. Phillip found that extremely frustrating.

Jackie's patience and Jennie Lou's calming qualities helped him find a way around his mental blocks, however. He was more able to participate thanks to them, and more able to express his love for his family.

Phillip had decided to come down the back stairs because he wanted to get Cynthia's Justin Bieber backpack. She loved it so much, and Phillip knew what it was like to want to use familiar things. Consequently, he was standing on the landing halfway up when Vincent passed the stairs, holding his gun. Vincent, focused on the voices he was hearing, never looked up the stairs, and never saw Phillip.

Phillip had a hatred for Vincent, not because Vincent had aimed that same gun at him days earlier, but because he had caused such grief and worry for Jackie, Mike Woods, and the other kids. That hatred gave Phillip some needed clarity and focus.

Phillip wanted Vincent out of his house.

Phillip was strong.

And Vincent didn't know Phillip was behind him.

Phillip gently put down the two suitcases, and began easing down the stairs. At the bottom, he peered around the door facing.

Vincent was just bringing his gun up, aiming at the people in the front hall.

Phillip hurriedly came up behind Vincent, and hit the unsuspecting man in the back of the head, with his hand, as hard as he could. When Vincent hit the floor across the hall, Phillip followed.

VINCENT, STUNNED, COULDN'T figure out why people were shouting at him, or why they were calling him "Phillip". He was on his hands and knees, shaking his head to clear it.

Suddenly, Vincent felt a hand on his collar, and he was hoisted into the air and held there, with his toes just barely above the floor. He looked at what was holding him, and a small, cold finger of fear traveled along his body as his mind cleared.

Phillip was holding Vincent by the collars of both his shirt and sport coat. Vincent had time to think about the incredible strength required to hold a one-hundred-eighty-pound man off the floor. Vincent was facing the front of the house. He could see five guns pointed at him. Looking down at Phillip, Vincent saw that Phillip had no expression on his face, but the boy's eyes held a killing hatred.

"Hold on, big boy," said Vincent. "Let's talk this over, okay?"

Then, Vincent did the only thing he could.

He kicked Phillip in the balls, as hard as he could.

Phillip immediately dropped Vincent. Vincent wasted no time, and ran for the back door, counting on the fact that the boy was blocking any gunfire.

Vincent wanted to get to his car, and quickly. He had more guns there.

"BRANDON! PATTY! CATCH that son of a bitch!" shouted Joey, as they all rushed to Phillip.

Brandon and Patty ran out the back door after Vincent.

Louie was the first to reach Phillip. He put his hand on the boy's shoulder. "Hey, son. It hurts, real bad, don't it? I know, I been there." Louie patted Phillip. "Dat was a brave thing you did, son, but it was dangerous as hell. If you had gotten hurt, I never would have forgiven myself. Don't do nuthin' like that again, you hear?"

Tears were streaming from Phillip's eyes. He was lying in a fetal position, hands tucked between his legs, covering his aching testicles. "Bad guy...was gonna...shoot. Hate him!" said Phillip, between clenched teeth.

"You've seen him before, then?" asked Jessica.

Phillip nodded.

"Is he the one that was with Jackie?"

Again, Phillip nodded.

Jessica looked up at Joey. "I'll stay with him, if you and Louie want to help Patty and Brandon."

Mike pushed Jennie Lou close to Phillip, then knelt beside the big boy. "Jen and I , we got him. Thanks," he said to Jessica.

"No need to help us, sir," said Patty from the back door. "The man had a car parked on the next street. He got away."

"Sorry, sir," Brandon said to Joey.

Joey shook his head. "It's my own fault. I should have put somebody by the back door. I wasn't expecting that. Jennie Lou, was that the guy that Jackie called 'Vincent'?"

"Yes, sir."

"Hey, Joey," called Louie from a few feet away. "He left us a present." Louie pointed to the stainless steel handgun.

"Good. Let's bag it and tag it," said Joey. "It'll make a nice gift for Mr. Yates. If Phillip can walk, people, let's get out of here, and we'll have Caleb check him out when we get back to the building." Joey headed toward the front door, stopped, and turned to face Brandon. "He outran *you?*"

Brandon rolled his eyes upward and spread his hands in a "Stuff Happens" gesture.

WHEN VINCENT KNOCKED on the door to Mickey Giambini's office, he felt an icy finger of fear down his back. He had never before failed in carrying out an assignment from his boss before, but he had seen what happened to others that failed.

Vincent entered the office when he heard the "Come in!" from inside. Leo Lesko was sitting in one of the chairs facing Giambini's desk. Giambini had a huge smile on his face.

"Vincent!" said Giambini. "Look who's back from Vegas!" He gestured to Lesko. "And with good news, too! Tell him, Leo!"

Lesko smiled and said, "I went to talk to the guys in Vegas about that bet Mickey made. I told them that if, officially, the fight never took place, then the bet never took place. You can't bet on something that didn't happen. Since it didn't happen, the money should be returned." He spread his hands. "The Vegas boys agreed. We got back our money."

Vincent had sat down in the second chair in front of Giambini's desk while Lesko explained. "That's good news, boss."

Giambini smiled. "You betcher ass it's good news! It means that the pressure's off. We got money, and we're back where we started from before the fight. So we got a lifetime to get the Belew dame to...increase our fortunes, so to speak." He pointed at Vincent. "Hey, did you kill one of the kids like I toldja?"

Vincent took a deep breath. "No, sir."

Lesko showed surprise, and the smile fell from Giambini's face.

"You're kiddin', right?" asked Giambini. "You ain't *never* let me down before! Ain't that right, Leo?"

Lesko nodded. "You're right, boss."

Giambini looked at Vincent. "You gotta reason for not killing one of them brats, Vincent?"

Vincent nodded.

"Then, by all means," said Giambini, leaning back in his office chair. "Explain yourself."

Vincent described the events at the house. At the mention of Joey Justice and Louie Washington, both Lesko and Giambini showed interest. When Vincent explained about being cold-cocked from behind and losing his favorite weapon, Lesko winced and Giambini shook his head in sympathy. When he described how he had escaped, the other two men nodded.

"Sounds like it was a narrow thing," said Giambini.

Vincent nodded. "It was, Mr. Giambini."

"What I wanna know," said Giambini speculatively, "is how Justice Security is involved in this."

"Yeah," replied Lesko. "What's a two-bit security company buttin' into something like this?"

Giambini shot a look at Lesko. "I wouldn't call them 'two-bit', Leo. They sent Fernandez runnin' with his tail between his legs."

"Yeah, but he'll be back, Mickey," replied Lesko. "Probably worse than before."

Vincent looked at Giambini. "Boss, I'm sorry I messed up."

Giambini waved a hand at Vincent. "Ahhhh, don't worry about it, Vincent. Circumstances were beyond your control. You didn't know." He leaned forward and put an arm on his desk. "But I wanna know why they were there. And I know who to ask."

Vincent smiled at his boss. "Let's go ask her, boss."

DR. CALEB MITCHELL pronounced Phillip physically okay. "They're gonna throb for a couple of days. I recommend some ice to keep the swelling down." He turned to Joey. "Seriously, Joey, you really need to consider hiring a medical doctor and installing him on staff here. I can do minor things, but if something major comes up, we're screwed."

Joey nodded. "Working on it, Caleb, I promise. Jessica, can you round up the children? If Yates is prompt, he's probably here already. Bring them to the situation room in twenty minutes, please." Joey left the room and headed for the main lobby.

Once in the main lobby, Joey stepped up to the reception desk. Tony Armstrong was there.

"Tony," said Joey. "I need fifty grunts here tomorrow morning by nine o'clock. I'll explain their assignments tomorrow, but they'll be working in pairs."

"Will do, Joey," replied Tony. "Where do you want them to gather?"

"Hmmm...I guess have them here. I'll speak to them in the cafeteria."

"You have a visitor," said Tony, gesturing to a nondescript man of average height, dressed in an off-the-rack black suit. "He's FBI, and his name is John Yates."

"I was expecting him, Tony," replied Joey. "Thanks."

Joey walked over to Yates, and held out his hand to shake hands with the FBI man as he stood.

"Mr. Yates?" Joey said.

Yates nodded.

"Joey Justice. Thank you for coming on such short notice, sir."

"Marcus Moore made it sound like a royal summons," replied Yates with a hint of sarcasm.

Joey smiled, and gestured toward the elevators. "This way, please, Mr. Yates."

As the two men walked, Joey addressed Yates's comment. "Marcus is used to things happening quickly with our company. We're unconventional, and we don't do things the way people like you think we should. We get results, and Marcus knows that." Joey stopped, and turned to face Yates. His anger and frustration with the FBI man was evident. "Mr. Yates, I could spend hours trying to convince you that your time with us is well-spent. I could make phone calls to levels of government that would make you shiver in your wingtips and force you to help us. I choose instead to trust you, as my friend Marcus Moore asked me to do, and like he asked *you* to do. If you want to turn this into a pissing contest, I would rather take Mickey Giambini on *without* your help. *Choose*, sir. Now. Before I waste any more time with you." Joey crossed his arms, waiting.

For his part, Yates stood tall and met Joey's look straight-on. "There are some, Mr. Justice, that say you are a showboat. Others are saying that your little run-in with Esteban Fernandez was totally unnecessary, almost caused a great loss of life, and may yet prove to be a source of danger to innocent people. Many in the Bureau are proud of you, because you *do* achieve results. Marcus warned me that our personalities would clash. Our personalities are irrelevant, Mr. Justice. We do not need to like each other to work together. However, if you expect special privileges from me, or expect me to be at your beck and call whenever you choose, or if you expect me to help you break the law, I will not. I am a Federal agent, and you would do well to remember that. With those ground rules, I 'choose' to assist you, sir. Now," Yates gestured toward the elevators as he spoke, "may we continue, before I waste any more time with you?"

Joey met Yates's stare for several seconds with no expression on his face. Then he half-smiled, punched the elevator button, and said, "Agreed, Mr. Yates."

As the doors opened, Joey gestured politely and said, "You may enter the royal conveyance, sir." Yates shot a look at Joey, who chose to ignore it.

ON THE FOURTH FLOOR, the elevator doors opened onto a cacophony of voices and activitiy. Turk was standing behind the reception desk, with Tommy tucked under one arm. Turk was pointing to Nicky, who was standing in the corner of the room beside the elevators, and Misty was heading toward the boy with a dark look in her eyes. Cynthia was sitting in one of the reception chairs with a smirk that could only be worn by the innocent.

Tommy was screaming, "Let me go, you big ape!" and wiggling in Turk's arms. Turk was saying, "He's over there, Misty!" Nicky was saying, "What did I do?" to Misty, who replied, "If you think *that* was funny, let me show *you* a practical joke or two, young man!" Cynthia started giggling at Misty's remark.

"Oh, crap," said Joey. He ran off the elevator and intercepted Misty.

"Honey, what's wrong?" asked Joey.

Misty was struggling to get past Joey. "Let me GO, Joey! That boy's butt needs to meet my hand *NOW!*"

Joey said, "But, what did he *do?*"

Misty stopped struggling. "Both boys need a good spanking! Oh, it was well thought out, I have to give them that! They must have done it before, the little *rats!*"

"What?" said Joey.

Misty took a breath. "Cynthia said that she had to use the bathroom, and asked if I would help her. Well, of course I'm going to help her, right? We were looking at the situation room, so Tommy starts asking me questions. He was the distraction, while Nicky disappeared. I didn't think anything of it, until Cynthia said that the problem had become a prairie dog. We fly into the ladies' room, and Cynthia barely makes it to the toilet in time. Well, she accomplishes what she needs to do. One problem: her toilet paper roll is *soaked!* You couldn't pry off any of it in one piece! So, I check the other stall, and that roll of paper is soaked, too! So is every roll of paper in the storage area under the sink, and the paper towels are *gone!* I ducked into the men's room, and met Nicky coming out. When I saw that the toilet paper in the men's room was watered down, too, I put two and two together. Turk had some napkins left from lunch, so I took care of Cynthia and brought her out here. Turk caught Tommy for me, but Nicky slipped away from him. That's when *you* came in!" She glared at Joey and crossed her arms defiantly. "So, you're home now...*you* deal with them!"

Joey was trying not to laugh. He knew if he laughed, the boys had won...and Misty would probably hurt him. When he had control of himself, he said, "Turk, please put Tommy down. Tommy, come over here."

Tommy walked over and stood beside Nicky. "Boys, did you wet down the toilet paper in the bathrooms?"

Both boys were looking down at the carpet. "Yes, sir," they said in unison.

Joey almost lost it again. Again, he got himself under control. "I'm ashamed of you. How could you do that to your sister?" He got not answer from the boys. "Okay, here's what's going to happen as punishment. Turk, what's the cleaning schedule for the restrooms on this floor?"

"Three times a day," said Turk. "Eight in the morning, two in the afternoon, and again at eight at night."

"You two are going to be the bathroom janitors for the next week for this floor," said Joey.

Tommy said, "Awww, maaannn!", while Nicky said, "No way, man!"

Joey cocked his head as if he wasn't sure of what he heard. "Excuse me, did I hear one of you say, 'No way'?"

Nicky nodded and looked up. "Yeah, I did. We hired *you*, man! We tell *you* what to do, not the other way." He crossed his arms defiantly. "I'm not gonna do it. You got no right. You can't make me."

Tommy smacked Nicky on the arm. "Shut *up*, Nicky! You're gonna make it worse!"

"*Naw*, Tommy! He can't make us do nothin'! He don't have any right!"

Joey nodded, as if understanding what Nicky was saying. "So, Nicky...you don't think that I have the right to discipline you?"

Nicky nodded, smirking. "That's *right*, Mr. Joey Justice."

"Turk!"

"Yes, boss."

"Did that paper from the governor's office get here yet?"

"Got it right here, boss."

"Would you hand it to me? And page Jessica to bring Phillip and Jennie Lou up here immediately."

Turk paged Jessica, then took the governor's envelope to Joey. Turk was chuckling under his breath. As executive secretary, he had already read it.

Joey turned to Yates, who was standing in front of the elevator, smiling at the situation. "Mr. Yates, I apologize for the delay in our talk. If you'd be so kind as to sit down next to Cynthia? Part of what I need to talk to you about will be in this paper."

Yates smiled. "I'm a father myself, Mr. Justice. I understand completely." He sat down next to Cynthia, who smiled up at the FBI man. He smiled back.

The elevator door opened, and Jessica stepped out with Phillip, followed by Louie pushing Jennie Lou's wheelchair. Mike Woods stepped out last.

"We're not late, so something is obviously up," said Jessica.

"Yeah, what's happenin', Joe?" said Louie.

"I need to talk to the kids for a minute," said Joey. "But, first, I'll let Misty tell you what Tommy and Nicky did."

Misty told them. Jessica shot the boys a fierce look, but Louie and Mike were having trouble keeping straight faces. Louie had put one hand over his mouth to help control his smile, while Mike's face was beet red.

Joey then told them what he had decided about an appropriate punishment, and Nicky's feelings about it. "Young Mr. Watson feels that since you children hired me, that he should be telling me what to do, not the other way around. So, I wanted all of you here to hear what this paper says. Please gather around. Phillip, do you feel up to helping Cynthia, big guy?"

Cynthia turned to Yates and said, "Excuse me, sir," as she got out of her chair. Phillip held out a steadying hand for her, then both made their way over to the corner. Louie pushed Jennie Lou closer to Joey.

"Children, Mr. Woods, please pay attention. This is from the governor's office, sent at my request today," said Joey. "The first page is a letter from the governor explaining that the enclosed paper should take care of any questions about the welfare of you children. The second paper says, simply, 'Per the request of the office of the Governor and the Commissioner of the State Department Of Children's Services, be it known that the welfare of the minor children Phillip Wheeler, Jennie Lou Gwin, Tommy Larkin, Nicky Watson, and Cynthia Rudisill shall be shared with equal responsibility by Jacqueline Belew and Joey Justice.' And the proclamation is signed by a State Judge.'" He lowered the paper and looked at the children. "Congratulations, kids. I'm your temporary foster parent."

Four of the five children had their mouths open, and were looking at Joey and Misty with total surprise. Phillip was smiling, and, for once, was not rocking.

"Mr. Mike Woods," said Joey. Mike looked up. "This does *not* mean that Jackie isn't capable. Or that you aren't capable. I did this so that I can be financially and parentally responsible for these children. But, as their foster parent, I can see that everything that *can* be medically done to improve these children's lives *will* be done. I do *not* take the job of being a parent lightly."

Mike nodded. "Understood, Joey. Thank you for your generosity."

Joey waved it off. He then squatted down to Nicky's level and said, "What were you saying about not having the right to tell you what to do?"

Cynthia broke the silence. "So, that means you're our foster dad?"

"Sure does, sweetheart," said Joey.

Cynthia hobbled over to him. "Will you hug me?"

Joey smiled, and wrapped the little girl in his arms. "You *bet* I will, little girl."

Tommy looked at Joey. "So you're our foster dad?"

Joey nodded.

"You know what? You are the *coolest*!" said Tommy, as he launched himself into Joey's arms.

Nicky still had his arms crossed. "So you think that a paper makes you a dad?"

Joey stood up straight and looked into Nicky's eyes. "No," he replied, after a moment of consideration. "The paper makes me *legally* responsible. Day-to-day care makes a dad." He gestured to Mike Woods. "*There* is a dad. He loves all of you. And *that* is something that money can't buy." Joey squatted to Nicky's level. "But, I care a great deal about all of you, and the first thing we're gonna do is to have your polio checked, Tommy and Jennie Lou will also undergo the best medical attention available. Cynthia will be checked out by the best CP doctors that can be found, and Phillip will be evaluated to see if we can help his autism. Anything that *can* be helped, *will* be helped. In the meantime, I still think that a week's worth of toilet cleaning will make you think twice in the future about pulling practical jokes." He looked up at Mike. "Do you agree, Mike?"

Mike nodded. "Sounds like a plan to me, Joey."

Joey looked back at Nicky. "So there you have it. Both dads think you should clean toilets for a week. You'll start tonight." He stood up. "Now, will you all please come with Mr. Yates and I to the situation room?"

As the procession headed down the hall, Joey turned to Turk.

"Turk, please coordinate with Caleb, and find the best doctors in the country that specialize in each of these kids' problems. I want appointments no later than Wednesday for all of them."

"Will do, boss."

"Thanks, big guy."

Joey went down the hall to the situation room. Everyone had found seats, with the exception of Phillip. Phillip stood beside Jennie Lou's wheelchair, rocking slowly. Joey patted the boy on the shoulder lightly as he went to an empty chair at the round table.

"For those of you that don't know this gentleman, Marcus Moore sent him to us," said Joey. "His name is John Yates, and he's the FBI's lead person on mob activity in the city." Joey turned to Jennie Lou and said, "Jennie, please tell Mr. Yates what you told me this morning, and what brought you to us."

JACKIE TURNED OUT HER light and laid back on her small bed. Her mind was reeling, and her face hurt from two backhand slaps from Vincent.

Vincent, Giambini, and Lesko had just left. She had not answered their questions, but the questions themselves told her what she wanted to know.

"Why would these kids hire Justice Security?" they wanted to know. "What does Justice Security know about us?" "Is all this a setup?"

The main thing that made her happy was that the kids had done what she told them, and that Justice Security was coming to rescue her.

WHEN THE KIDS HAD FINISHED their part, Joey, Louie, Misty, and Jessica took up the story, and brought the FBI specialist up to speed on the events of that morning.

"So, Mr. Yates," said Joey, "here's the gun we recovered." Joey gave Yates a sealed plastic bag containing the stainless steel gun that Vincent had dropped. "We could have processed it here, and actually accessed the Bureau's database to compare the fingerprints, but we thought it might benefit all of us if you process the weapon at *your* lab. Other than that, do you have any questions? Or suggestions? We're open to both!"

Yates found himself reeling at the story, and at Justice Security. Marcus Moore had been right in his description of the people at this company, in that he had said that trouble seemed to find them...but, usually, trouble regretted choosing them. He spoke his next sentences carefully.

"It would seem that the man you stopped today may be Vincent Lambosa," Yates said. "Lambosa is one of Giambini's top men, and you were extremely lucky to have caught him by surprise today." He looked around the table. "I promise you, he won't forget it, either. Whoever stopped him...well, let's just say that Lambosa won't take it well." He held up the plastic bag. "You folks realize that it's two-thirty on a Friday afternoon?" Everyone nodded. "The lab won't have enough time to process this weapon before Monday. Are you sure you want to wait that long? As a private company, your 'go-home' times don't dictate what work gets done."

Joey stared at the table for a moment, then looked to his partners, as if for confirmation. When he turned back to Yates, he said, "We'll agree, on one condition, Mr. Yates. You must stay with the gun throughout the processing. If you'll do that, we'll jump on it today."

Yates thought about it. Here was a chance to bring down Mickey Giambini, if he was willing to work with a civilian company to do it. *And I firmly believe that Joey Justice is the man to do it!*

"Mr. Justice," said Yates, "you have a deal."

Jessica had agreed to roust the lab techs and stay with Yates during the processing of the gun. Louie had agreed to take over watching the children for a while. Turk agreed to stay later to help with decisions to be made after the lab finished their work.

Joey and Misty went to their shared apartment on the sixth floor for a few private moments. What started as a kiss at the door turned into a slow, sweet lovemaking session.

Afterward, as they snuggled each other, they talked.

"Joey?" said Misty.

"Mmmm?"

"Dexter and Megan will be back on Monday."

"Yeah."

"Do you ever think about getting married?"

"Do you mean eloping, like they did?"

Misty thought for a minute. "Not necessarily. I mean, just getting married in general."

It was Joey's turn to think for a minute. "Yeah, I do. But it's like subconscious thinking, you know? It's always in the back of my mind."

She nodded. "I know what you mean, lover. It's always in the back of my mind, too."

"Are you thinking that you and I should get married?"

"Well...I've always thought we would...and we've been together for over ten years, Joey." She raised her head to look into his eyes. "Most couples have already been married for quite some time once they've been together that long." She half-smiled. "Some even have children."

Joey smiled back. "Really? Children?"

Misty playfully hit his chest. "Stop making fun! If you don't want to marry me, say so!"

"Seriously, Misty...do you think it's safe? Or fair? I mean, I'm not the only one that has a price on his head. Fernandez made it pretty clear that he wants you, too...just not for the same reason."

Misty looked into Joey's eyes. "Joey. As long as we're in this business, there's *always* going to be somebody in the background, waiting to take us down. If we let threats and fears rule our personal lives, the bad guys have won already."

Joey thought for a minute. "Misty, I'm scared. I'm scared of what would happen if some of these bad guys decided to take you as a hostage to me. I'm pretty sure I'd lose control of myself. And if something happened to you, I'd lose all reason to carry on. I'd probably just drink myself into a stupor, and go off somewhere alone to do it."

"Honey, I'd be the same way. But, remember what I said...if we let our fears control our lives..."

"Well, then...in that case..." He looked into her eyes. "Are you ready?"

Misty thought for a moment, then nodded.

"Okay, then...Misty, will you marry me?"

"No."

"SO, THE GUN IS DIRECTLY linked to Vincent Lambosa," said Yates.

Jessica gestured to the computer screen. "See for yourself. The FBI computer doesn't lie."

Yates shook his head in amazement. "So, let's run it through the national ballistics program, and see if there's a match."

Jessica pulled the keyboard over and started to type.

NICKY AND TOMMY WERE inside the boys' apartment, playing video games.

"Tommy," said Nicky.

"What?" replied Tommy, focused on the game.

Nicky put down his game controller. "Let's go explore."

"No way. You already got us in enough trouble."

"Come *on*, Tommy! Phillip's taking a nap, he won't know!"

"Uh-uh."

"Man, this is *Justice Security!* There's *gotta* be all *kinds* of neat stuff here to play with! Come on!"

Tommy put down his controller. "Ten minutes, Nicky. Ten minutes, then back here. I don't want that big guy...Turk...mad at me, man."

Nicky grinned and put out his hand. "*Deal,* brother!"

They shook hands and crept quietly out into the hall.

"NO?" ASKED JOEY.

"No." Misty replied.

Joey looked surprised and puzzled. "But...all that talk...why, Misty?"

"Joey, I love you with all that I am," said Misty. "But, if I have to *talk you into* marrying me, I don't want to marry you."

"You are *not* 'talking me into' marrying you!"

"Oh, so you don't want to marry me at all?"

"What?"

"You just said that I wasn't talking you into marrying me."

"But...you said...I just..."

"And, to me, that means you don't want to marry me." She sat up and threw her legs over the edge of the bed. As she turned her face away from him, she smiled to herself at his confusion.

Joey sat up, reached out, and put his hands on her bare shoulders. "Misty, please listen to me. I love you with all my heart, and I really want to marry you. Whenever and wherever you want to marry me, I'll marry you. And I'll love you for rest of my life." He wrapped his arms around her chest and pulled her close. "Please marry me, Misty. Please be my wife."

Misty put her hand over his and laid her head on his arm. "Well, since you put it that way...yes. I will marry you, Joseph James Justice."

The private phone, reserved for partner-to-partner conversations, rang. It was Jessica, calling them to the situation room.

CYNTHIA AND JENNIE Lou were relaxing in their suite, chatting with Patty Ferguson, who had volunteered to stay with the girls for the time being.

It was Patty who answered the phone. It was Jessica, asking if the children and Mr. Woods could be brought to the situation room. Patty said she'd take care of it.

Patty told the girls what was going on, and asked them to get ready. She then called Mike Woods, and he said that he'd head down shortly.

As the girls got ready, Patty went next door to get the boys. All she found was Phillip. She immediately called the front desk and informed Tony Armstrong that Nicky and Tommy were AWOL. Tony notified Turk by radio. Turk said that he was on it.

IN THE GYM, THE PHONE on the wall rang. Louie was working on the weight machine, and was quite expressive when he had to stop to answer it.

It was Jessica, calling him to the situation room.

TOMMY AND NICKY HAD made it to the lobby by taking the elevator to the second floor, then taking the stairs. Using stairs was a tricky affair for both boys, because of their leg braces, but they accomplished it with no mishaps.

They opened the stairwell door to the lobby. They saw no one, and began quietly creeping out into the lobby proper. When the door shut, both boys jumped and turned to look behind them.

Turk stood two feet behind them with his big arms crossed and a huge scowl on his face.

"Aw, *man!*" said Nicky, as Turk reached for them.

"MR. YATES, I UNDERSTAND your desire to question this Vincent person," Misty was saying. "Our argument is that if you pick him up before we retrieve Miss Belew, you could jeopardize our chances of getting her out unharmed."

"What's happenin'?" said Louie, as he entered the situation room.

"Fingerprints on the gun match Lambosa," said Jessica. "Then, we ran the ballistics through the national database, and we got five hits."

"*Five?*" asked Louie incredulously.

"Five," said Jessica, nodding. "One of them matched a murder on the same street as the Belew house."

"Mrs. Morgan," whispered Jennie Lou.

Jessica nodded. "That's the one, sweetheart. Did you know her?"

"Only to speak to...we didn't know her well. She didn't approve of us," replied Jennie Lou. "I mean, she liked us. She just didn't approve of Jackie taking care of us alone. Not married."

"Well, she's answering to her own judgement right now, courtesy of Vincent Lambosa," said Jessica.

"And our FBI friend wants to go pick him up. Now," said Joey.

Louie looked at Yates. "Ma-an, you crazy! Didn't you promise Joey that you'd let him work this case his way?"

"I did," replied Yates. "But that was before the tests were run, and everything checked out. Ballistics matched several murders, and his fingerprints matched. That's good enough for me. I'm picking him up and charging him."

"What are you planning to charge him with?" asked Joey calmly.

"Murder. Racketeering. Attempted murder. Kidnapping. Lots of things!"

"And what is your evidence?" asked Joey again.

Yates looked at Joey as if he had grown horns and bleated. Then, slowly, realization and suspicion grew, and his look changed. "You did something with that weapon, didn't you?"

"We put it safely back into our arsenal downstairs, freshly polished, cleaned, and oiled," said Joey, with a slight smile. "We even re-rifled the barrel, to give each bullet a nice, new design when it's fired."

"You son of a bitch!" shouted Yates, as he banged his fist onto the table. "I could arrest you right now for destroying evidence!"

"What evidence, Mr. Yates? Of your own knowledge, do you know where that gun came from?"

Yates, furious, hissed, "No!"

"It was one of ours, for all you know."

Yates was spluttering. "But...I got...I saw the match on the fingerprints! And the damn ballistics *matched that gun!* And the computers at the Bureau will show that you entered the system, and what you looked at! You are going *down,* Justice! Tampering with evidence – especially evidence as hot as this – is a major crime!"

Joey was drawing circles on the table with his forefinger. "Mr. Yates, I employ a *lot* of specialists in this company. Two of my partners, Dexter Beck and his wife Megan, are the best computer hackers I've ever seen. I also have on staff three computer hackers that were formerly employed by the FBI. I promise you that your computers will show that we have not been in your system since Fernandez was here. And, as far as what you say that you saw, no one here knows what you're talking about." He leaned forward in his chair, until his face was three inches from the FBI man's. "There was *no* gun, there were *no* tests, and there was *no* match of fingerprints or ballistics." He leaned back. "I was wrong to ask you here, sir. I apologize for wasting your time." Joey stood. "Now, if you will come with me, Mr. Yates, my friend Louie will assist me in escorting you from the premises."

Yates's mouth had been open in disbelief. As he realized that he had nothing, he closed his mouth with a snap and stood. He straightened his coat, then his tie, and walked stiffly out of the situation room. He continued down the hall to the elevators. Joey and Louie were to his left and right, respectively. The executive lobby was empty. Yates pressed the down button.

As Yates waited, he rocked back and forth on his feet. "You haven't heard the last of this, Justice."

"I disagree, Mr. Yates," replied Joey. "You should have trusted us. You would have had a career-making bust if you had cooperated. Now, you'll have to live with your choice, and you will not be on hand to witness Giambini's tumble, or Lambosa's downfall. Regrettable, sir."

Yates turned to Louie. "You heard all that, I'm sure."

Louie stuck a finger in his right ear and wiggled it. "You know, since that damn boxin' match, I ain't been able to hear a damn thang. I need to get it checked out, I guess." He put his hand down and looked at Yates. "I will make a couple of observations, however." His language had become clipped, and carried clear enunciation. This was a sure way to know that Louie had become angry. "Trust is a fragile thing. Once broken, it is very hard to mend. The other thing is, a man that can't keep his word isn't much of a man."

The elevator opened, and Turk stood inside. He had Tommy under one arm and Nicky under the other.

"Caught 'em, boss. Where do you want 'em?"

Joey glanced at his wristwatch. "It's close enough to eight o'clock. Turk, please supervise them as they clean the bathrooms on this floor."

"Glad to, boss," replied Turk with a smile. He stepped off of the elevator, and the other men stepped on.

Nothing else was said from any of the three. Yates was escorted out the front door.

"What was that all about, Joe? Why kinda bullshit was that guy up to?" asked Louie.

Joey was pulling out his cell phone. He held up a finger. "Can you wait until we get back upstairs, Louie? I got calls to make, quickly."

Louie shrugged as Joey speed-dialed.

"Computer lab."

"This is Joey. I need a cleanup."

"Sure, boss, what and when?"

Joey told them to clean all traces of any usage of the FBI computer that day. "And I mean not so much as a *hint* of rain in the cloud, okay?" That meant leave *no* traces.

Next, he dialed the lab. When they answered, he told them to send that test gun to the armory, with instructions to clean it, oil it, polish it, and re-rifle the barrel.

"Sure, Joey. When do you want it done?"

"Yesterday," replied Joey. He hung up, and immediately dialed a longer number. He reflected that not everyone had the private cell phone number of the Director of the FBI...When the man answered, Joey identified himself, asked after the Director's health, then explained his reason for calling, while he and Louie got onto the elevator. He had asked Marcus Moore to recommend someone to offer advice on mob activity, because Joey had a case that might lead to some racketeers. When John Yates had arrived that afternoon, he had listened to their story calmly enough, but had then began ranting about guns and fingerprints of someone they had never heard of, murders, and ballistics tests. Yes, in Joey's opinion, the man was overworked...perhaps the stress of his current assignment was more than the man could handle. Yes, Joey could see recommending an extended vacation...perhaps a reassignment to a less stressful position would be in order.

"Thank you, Director," said Joey into the phone as he winked at Louie. "Yes, sir. I'll certainly tell him. Take care, sir." Joey disconnected the call. "The Director said to tell you that you fought a great fight."

Louie shook his head. "What de hell's goin' on, Joey? What got into that guy? Didn't he understand that it was our case all the way through?"

Joey shook his head. "I don't know, Louie. All I'm sure of is that if that idiot picks up Lambosa now, Jackie's survival chances become extremely slim. Remember – *Lambosa saw us at Jackie's house.* He's bound to have shared that information with Giambini. Risking one person's life to score an arrest just doesn't seem right to me...especially when it isn't necessary, and could wait for a few days."

The elevator had opened, and Joey and Louie walked past Turk. He was sitting in front of the open door of the ladies rest room, smiling smugly as he watched Nicky and Tommy clean the inside. The two men continued down the hall to the situation room. When they walked in, everyone turned to look at them.

"The FBI man has been...dismissed...from the case," said Joey.

"Why, Joey?" asked Cynthia.

Joey smiled and hugged the girl close to him. "Because he wanted to put your foster mom's life in danger, sweetie." He sat down at the round table, and so did Louie. "Here's what happened with him, and why I did what I did..." Joey explained his thinking and why he felt that arresting Lambosa would put Jackie's life in danger. "So, he had to be gotten rid of. I wish we could have worked with him, but every FBI man isn't Marcus."

"So, what's the plan of action now, Joey?" asked Jessica.

"Tony is having fifty grunts here in the morning at nine o'clock," said Joey. "Then, Misty and I will take them and..." He told them all the rest.

Chapter 9

Saturday morning, fifty uniformed Justice Security members were in place in the cafeteria. Included in the fifty were Brandon King and Patty Ferguson. Both had volunteered for the job when they found out it was related to what had happened at the kids' house yesterday.

Tony Armstrong came into the "caff" and got everyone's attention.

"Good morning, people," said Tony.

Variations of the greeting came from around the room.

"I want each of you to fortify yourselves with whatever you normally have in the mornings, be it breakfast, or just coffee, or juice...or green cow patties, if that's what floats your boat," continued Tony among the chuckles around the room. "I just want you all to be on your toes and frosty for today. You're all going out with the big man today. He and Misty will fill you all in around nine fifteen, after their nine o'clock meeting upstairs. Some of you have seen the kids running around the building...be nice to them. They're our clients, and Joey is their foster father. The case you'll be assisting with involves finding these kids' foster mom. It could be dangerous, but not as dangerous as our recent dance with Fernandez. At least, I hope it isn't. If you all stick with your training and do what you're supposed to, everyone should be okay." He waved toward the buffet tables. "So get whatever you want, and relax for a bit. The big man will be down shortly." Tony stood. "Make me proud of the two-tone today, okay?" he said, referring to the two-toned brown uniforms all Justice Security grunts wore.

"...AND THAT'S ALL I GOT for today," said Louie, upstairs in the situation room. "Joe, you sure you and Misty don't want me or Jessica goin' wit' you today?"

Joey shook his head. "No, but thank you. I really need to have you two watching the kids today. With you two, I don't have to worry about them."

"Besides, if Joey's plan works, we won't have any results today," said Misty. "We're mostly putting people into position."

"I hope it works," said Jessica.

Joey and Misty got up to leave.

"Me, too," said Joey.

"Oh, by the way," said Misty from the door. Louie and Jessica looked at them. "Joey and I are engaged."

They left their friends sitting speechless.

THE COUPLE SWUNG BY the front desk in the lobby on the way to the "caff".

"Is everyone here, Tony?" asked Misty.

"Good morning, bosses," said Tony cheerfully. "All fifty present and accounted for. They're waiting for you."

"Got those photos?" asked Joey.

"Sure do. Ready when you two are."

Joey smiled and nodded. "Good job, Tony."

"Thank you, sir."

The three people entered the caff. A few people were still getting their food and taking it back to their tables. Joey spotted Brandon and Patty, and waved at both.

Joey, Misty, and Tony stood at the side of the seating area, and Joey looked at Misty, who nodded.

"Good morning, people!" shouted Joey.

Loud shouts returned to him.

"Here's what today is all about," said Joey, not shouting, but loud enough to be heard by everyone. "We have a group of children with handicaps staying here in the building. They are our clients. We have been hired to retrieve their foster mom, Jacqueline Belew. She has been kidnapped by the Mickey Giambini crime family here in the city." Joey heard mumbles in the room. "We are going to attempt to get her back with a minimum of violence. I'm not saying there won't be any, but we're going to keep it to the minimum necessary to get Ms. Belew back. Now, one of the ways the Giambini family makes its money is through the old protection racket. That's where they force businesses into paying them a percentage of their gross income, and the mob offers 'protection' from harm. Businesses that don't buy in suddenly have things happen to them...they burn down in the middle of the night, or explosions destroy the storefronts. This is one thing we can do to put pressure on Giambini to release our clients' foster mom. We're going to make a tour of convenience stores today, and talk to managers, owners, clerks...anyone in the store, and we're going to show pictures of Ms. Belew and a man named Vincent Lambosa. If the people we talk to recognize them, we're going to post two of you in that store. Your job will be to provide security and protection for the store...but we're doing it for free. And when someone from Giambini comes around to collect their 'protection' money, you will invite that person to leave the store, either upright or lying down – the choice is theirs. Don't kill them. But, hurt them. Make them think twice about returning. And, make sure that they carry a message with them when they leave...and that message is to release Jacqueline Belew. Now, this is important: Once you've thrown out Giambini's collection thugs, you call Tony here and let him know. We will then ring that establishment with more of us than Giambini can count, and we will prevent anything from happening to that establishment." He paused for a moment. "People, this could be a dangerous thing. In some places, more than two of you may be required. Business hours may require more than two of you to cover it properly. I don't care, people will be there for you, if we have to put plainclothes personnel into two-tones for a few days. But, we are going to hurt this mobster's money, and will continue to do so until Ms. Belew is back with her family.

"Now, let's finish up our breakfast and get this done for these kids!"

TWO PASSENGER BUSSES left the Justice Security underground garage. Misty was in charge of one bus, with twenty-four uniforms, and Joey had the other bus, with twenty-six.

Guessing that Vincent had first spotted Jackie inside a convenience store, the plan was that Misty would start with convenience stores close to the Belew house and continue inward toward downtown. Joey would start with stores close to the Hollow, and work back toward their own building.

Misty's first stop was the little store closest to Jackie's house, which happened to be the store that Vincent took Jackie to that first day. She walked inside, and was greeted by Steve, who was working a Saturday in order to give his assistant a day off.

"Hi!" said Steve. "What can I help you with today?"

Misty held out her hand, and Steve shook it. "My name is Misty Wilhite. I'm with Justice Security, and I need your help."

Steve smiled. "I've heard of you, and your company. I was in the convention center the night of the fight. I understand I owe you folks my life."

Misty smiled modestly. "It was closer than the media was told. Joey and Jim Dandy were side-by-side trying to defuse the trigger, and it was strictly an accident that made it happen."

Steve shook his head. "What was that crazy man thinking?"

"We'll get him. Or he'll get us. In the meantime, we have another case that we're working on." She took out Jackie's picture. "Have you ever seen this woman?"

"Yeah, sure. That's Jacqueline Belew. She live just a couple of streets over, on Peach. Why are you interested in her?"

"We think she's been kidnapped by Mickey Giambini."

"The Mafia boss?"

Misty nodded.

"Wow! What does he want with Jackie?"

"He thinks she can make him some money. Her kids have hired us to find her, and bring her home." She slid over a photo of Vincent. "Have you ever seen this man?"

Steve nodded. "I have." He pointed to his left eye. The skin around it was a pale olive color. "He gave me this bruise, and a few others. He forced me to buy what he called 'insurance'. I went along because I didn't want anything to happen to my store. His name's Vincent something."

"Lambosa," said Misty.

Steve pointed at her. "Yeah, that's it."

"How much does he charge you, and how often do you have to pay it?"

Steve named a figure, then said, "He comes around once a week, on Saturday, to collect."

"Saturday?" asked Misty excitedly. "Has he been here yet?"

Steve shook his head. "Not yet. Why?"

"You've been coerced into a 'protection' racket," said Misty. "That brings me to what I want to talk to you about." She told him about protection rackets, and what Justice Security proposed to do about it, by putting monetary pressure onto Giambini. "So, we'd like to offer you uniformed security for the next two weeks, two armed people per shift, at no charge to you. I'd really like to have them in place before Lambosa shows up to collect. How about it, Steve?"

"Free?" asked Steve.

Misty nodded. "All that you will need from us for two weeks, absolutely free to you. After that, if you like what we do and want to continue having us around, we'll talk. And I promise you, it's way cheaper than Giambini!"

JOEY'S FIRST STOP RESULTED in sightings for Lambosa, but not for Jackie. However, they agreed to Joey's pitch, and he stationed two uniforms at the store.

Joey's second stop was *Kwikstuff.* Malik, the owner, was behind the register. He had to lay off one of his clerks in order to pay Vincent's protection money.

Joey introduced himself, and Malik recognized him.

"It is a great pleasure to meet you, Mr. Justice," he said, as he shook Joey's hand.

"I'm hoping you can help me, sir," said Joey. He handed Jackie's picture to Malik. "Have you ever seen this woman?"

Malik looked at Joey suspiciously. "Why do you ask?"

"She's missing, and we think that Mickey Giambini's people took her. We think that *they* think she can make them some money somehow."

Malik's eyes flashed. "Aaaaahhhh! I bet it's because of her winning all the time!"

Joey used his best poker face, but was extremely excited inside. "Oh, you mean the lottery thing!"

Malik began nodding. "Yes, yes. She *never* lost! Always, when I see her coming in, I know she is going to be winning money!"

Well, there's confirmation of the kids' story. "Have you ever seen this man?" He handed Malik the photo of Vincent.

Malik's face closed up immediately. "Why do you ask about this man?"

"This man's name is Vincent Lambosa," replied Joey. "We think that he had something to do with Jackie's kidnapping. Her foster kids have hired us to get her back."

"Mr. Justice, this man is evil," said Malik. Malik then told Joey what he knew about Jackie, Vincent, and the protection money. "I am in deep trouble. He asks for much money! I had to let one of my clerks go so that I could use that money to pay this evil man! And now you tell me that he has kidnapped Miss Jackie so that she can win more money for him and his boss! I want to help, Mr. Justice, but this man is too much for me. He has beaten me several times. I cannot do much."

"Let me show you what I can do to help you," said Joey. He then explained what Justice Security wanted to do for the next two weeks, and that it was all free. "After that two week free period, we go away. Or, if you like our service and security, you'll find that our rates are quite affordable. And, during those two weeks, we'll make sure that Lambosa doesn't bother you."

"Mr. Justice, you are a gift from Allah," said Malik. "Please. Bring your people inside. Tell them to make themselves at home!"

Joey stepped out to the bus and called Brandon and Patty outside.

"Okay, you two are stationed here, because this man has given me confirmation of the kids' stories, and has also given me a lot of information, and I want him to have the best. That's you two. You might get a second chance at Lambosa, so be frosty and ready to take on the world if need be. You have your radios, so if things get hairy, don't hesitate to call for backup. Most of all, guard the client...but guard yourselves and each other as well. Clear?"

Both Brandon and Patty said forcefully, "Yes, *sir!*"

MISTY WAS THROUGH WITH her placements by eleven-thirty, Joey by twelve. Both agreed to head back to the building, and plan from there.

VINCENT WAS MAKING his rounds, picking up his "insurance payments" from various establishments around town. He had a group of guys he trusted hitting most of the businesses today, even though Saturday usually wasn't the best day to collect.

Vincent decided to stop at *Kwikstuff*. He enjoyed making the camel jockey pay through the nose...and he enjoyed slapping him around afterwards. It was one of the pleasant joys of his position, and always improved his disposition and made his day better.

Malik was smiling as Vincent walked into the store. *That's okay – I'll knock that smile off of his face in a few minutes.* That thought made Vincent smile.

"Hello, you happy asshole," said Vincent through his smile. "Got my money?"

Malik smiled even broader. "No. There won't be any more money, sir. Not for you."

Vincent cocked his head as if he hadn't heard correctly. "*What* did you say? No money?"

Malik shook his head. "No money. Ever. Not for you."

Vincent actually chuckled. "You piece of shit, I'm gonna break some bones this time. You'll find some money."

"I don't think so," came from behind Vincent. It was followed by a powerful blow across his kidneys that made him fall to the floor, writhing in pain. When he looked up, he saw Patty Ferguson standing over him, with a wooden cop baton in one hand, and a taser in the other. She then put the taser on her belt and began twirling the baton almost like a set of numchucks. "Guess who's doing the protecting in this store now, asshole? That's right – Justice Security! And I get to be the one to give you the message to take back to your boss! But, first, I have a couple of more lessons in humility for you." The baton hit Vincent on the elbow, then on the knee. Vincent didn't even see the blows coming as the baton twirled and spun. He knew he couldn't grab the baton, so he did the next thing to cross his mind. He spun his legs around and knocked Patty to the ground. Then he jumped over on her so that he was straddling her, and he drew his new gun. Not quite as shiny as his other one, but he'd been looking forward to breaking this one in.

"Humility lesson for you, bitch," said Vincent, as he put the gun between her eyes. "I hate to kill you without fucking such a gorgeous piece, so we're gonna go into the back room for a while. I'm going to show you what kind of message I take to *my* boss!"

"Not while I'm around," said a voice behind him. Another baton hit Vincent's extended elbow, and the crack of the broken bone could be heard all over the store. Vincent dropped the gun and collapsed back onto the floor again. Brandon had his gun drawn and pointing unwaveringly at Vincent's forehead. "We meet again. You okay, Patty?"

Patty nodded and got to her feet. "Can we kill him?"

"No. Mr. Justice told us not to," replied Brandon, his eyes never leaving Vincent's. "Just so you know, Vincent, I want to kill you. Not for what you've done as a mobster, or what you've done to this poor shopkeeper. No. I want to kill you for laying your hands on this sweet woman. But, I'll have to be satisfied with breaking your elbow, because *our* boss said to rough you up and send you back to your boss with a message."

Vincent was cradling his broken arm, but his look of hatred would have melted plastic. "Yeah? So *what*, black boy? Tell me your message, then I'll give *you* one." Vincent's head suddenly rocked to the left, as Patty spin-kicked the mobster on his right ear. It took a second or two for the pain to register, but it was sharp and large when it did.

"Call him something racial again, and I might just have to risk losing my job," said Patty.

"That's called 'friendship', asshole," said Brandon. "See, Patty and me, we look out for each other. That's what friends are for."

Through his throbbing headache, Vincent hissed, "Well, ain't that sweet."

"Here's the message, Vincent Lambosa," said Brandon. "Tell Mickey Giambini that Joey Justice says to let Jacqueline Belew go. If he lets her go, we go no further. If he doesn't let Jacqueline Belew go free, it will cost him a *whole* lotta money. And maybe a whole lotta people." Brandon cocked his head. "Do you understand, Vincent?"

Vincent didn't say anthing.

Patty stomped on Vincent's shin. Not hard enough to break it, but hard enough so that Vincent know that she could if she chose.

"Okay, okay, I got the message!" yelled Vincent.

"One last thing, Vincent," said Brandon. "Don't come back to *Kwikstuff*. It's under the protection of Justice Security. Personally, if you do, I'll take that as a challenge. And, then, I'll kill you. *Capice?* Now, get out of here."

Vincent climbed unsteadily to his feet, still cradling his broken elbow, and limped out of the store.

TONY FLAGGED DOWN JOEY as he passed through the lobby.

"Hey, boss, Misty is waiting for you in the situation room. She says hurry, that it's already started," Tony said.

"On my way," replied Joey.

When he entered the situation room, he could hear Brandon's voice on the room's radio receiver. "...and then he just stood up and limped out. We haven't seen him since, but neither of us think he's done with us. We think he'll be back, and he might bring friends."

"Brandon, Joey just got here. Tell him what you told me," Misty said into the microphone.

"Hello, sir," said Brandon. "We just had positive contact with Lambosa." He then told Joey every detail of what happened at *Kwikstuff*. "Last we saw him, sir, he was cradling a broken elbow and limping out of the store."

"I'm having some backup sent there, Brandon," said Joey. "Tell Malik to please close the store temporarily until backup gets there." To Misty he said, "Honey, would you please call down to Tony and have him send ten grunts to back them up. Make sure they're armed to the teeth, with shotguns *and* handguns. Tell him I want them there *now!*"

"Will ten be enough?"

Joey nodded. "I think so. At least for now." Pressing the microphone key again, he said to Brandon, "Okay, Brandon, we have ten people on the way with weapons to back you and Patty up. Where are you? Is the store closed?"

"Sir, Mr. Malik wants to speak with you," replied Brandon.

There was silence, then an audible click could be heard, along with voices. "Then you just speak into it, sir." "Like theese?" "Yes, sir." "Hello, Mr. Justice? He is not hearing me, I don't know what is wrong with..." "You need to let go of the button to hear him, Mr. Malik." "Oh!" There was another click, then silence.

Joey took the opportunity. "Go ahead, Malik."

The click came again. "Why must I close, Mr. Justice? I am doing good business, and am feeling secure!" There was a couple of seconds of silence, then "Let go of the button, Mr. Malik." "Oh!"

"Malik, my people just roughed up one of the most dangerous men working for Mickey Giambini. They broke his elbow, and cost him some ego. And they did it in full view of you. You are someone that is supposed to be intimidated and frightened of this man. Because of what happened, he has to do something to scare you back into line, and he must do it quickly. Sending more men in to protect you and your store is just common sense. It might prevent something extremely violent from happening to you or to your store. The reason I want you to close is so that you can actually leave the premises until my people get there. Stores and things can be replaced, Malik. You can't. Do you understand?"

Click. "I understand, Mr. Justice. I will close immediately." There was the sound of breaking glass. "What was that, Brandon?" "Holy crap! It's a brick of C-4, and it..." The radio went dead.

Joey stood motionless, then slowly put his hand on Misty's shoulder. "Oh, my God," he said quietly.

Chapter 10

Giambini held the gun two inches from the bridge of Vincent's nose. "*Tell me why I shouldn't just kill your worthless ass right now! Come* on, *asshole! Why shouldn't I kill you?*"

Vincent sat motionless in Giambini's office, facing a gun in his face for the second time within an hour.

"Vincent, if you've ever valued your shitpoke life, you better give me a reason, because you just brought fuckin' Justice Security down on me...*and I'm not fuckin' happy about it!*" The more Giambini talked, the more he waved his hands...and that included the one with the gun in it. "Those bastards just took on Esteban Fernandez and lived to tell about it! Even *I'm* scared of that crazy sumbitch! They've got the fuckin' FBI in their vest pockets, and God only knows what's in that armory of theirs!" He leaned over until his face was two inches from Vincent's. "And what do you do? What does my 'great observer' do? He kidnaps a broad that tells her kids to hire Justice Security, then this 'great observer' blows up a store with some Justice Security people in it! Now, tell me, great observer: what do I do to get Justice Security off my back? *Huh?*"

Vincent was quiet.

"Yeah, that's what I thought. I can't let her go, 'cause she'll press kidnapping charges against me, and they'd stick. But, I can't just *kill* her, either, 'cause I'd *never* get those pukes off my ass then! So, here I am with my 'great observer', stuck between a fuckin' rock and a fuckin' hard place, all because he couldn't wait a coupla weeks to get even with some turban-wearing asshole in a convenience store!"

Giambini stopped, and looked into Vincent's eyes. "So, I gotta give 'em something, Vincent. Something that might take 'em off my back, you know?" He extended the gun again. "So long, Vincent. Nothing personal. It's just business."

"Boss, can I talk to you a minute before you kill him? I got an idea." asked Rizzo.

Giambini shrugged. "Okay, Rizzo. Don't go anywhere, Vincent." Giambini walked over to Rizzo, and the two men put their heads close together and began talking quietly. Vincent tried, but couldn't hear what was being said. Once, Giambini said, "You gotta be kiddin' me, Rizzo...tell me you're fuckin' kiddin'!" Then, they began murmuring again. Giambini said, "Okay, it just might work, Rizzo. We'll try it – what can it hurt?"

Giambini walked back over to Vincent. "Vincent, it's your lucky day. Apparently, you didn't kill anybody with that C-4! You just blew the shit outta that camel jockey's store. Check it out." Giambini clicked on a remote, and the television on the wall came to life.

An attractive brunette was speaking into a microphone. "...Malik, the store owner. Mr. Malik, can you describe what happened?"

The camera shifted to a two-shot with Malik standing beside the reporter. "Yes, Miriam, I can describe it. The two Justice Security guards had just run a mob collector out of my store. We were talking with Mr. Justice over the radio a few minutes later, when someone threw a brick of C-4 through the store window. It had a red flashing detonator. Patty Ferguson, one of the guards, quickly picked up the explosive and threw it back out the window just before it exploded. She saved us all!"

The reporter turned the microphone back to herself. "You said they ran a mob collector out of your store. Can you elaborate on that?"

The microphone flipped back to Malik. Behind the reporter and the store owner, flashing police and ambulance lights could be seen, with officers milling around the cars. "Well, I had been forced to pay protection money to the Mickey Giambini mob by a man named Vincent Lambosa. Lambosa was the man that Justice Security ran out of my store. They had to let him go, because they had a message to be delivered to Giambini."

Flip. "And what was that message, Mr. Malik?"

Flip. "It was for him to let..." But his comments faded away as the reporter ran toward Joey. She had spotted him standing alongside Misty near the ambulance in the background.

When she ran up onto Joey and Misty, she stopped, and her feet almost skidded out from under her. "I'm speaking now with Joey Justice and Misty Wilhite, both of Justice Security. Joey, what can you tell us about the explosion here and the implied mob connection?"

Joey looked at the reporter. "Hello, Miriam. Hi, Steve!" he said to the cameraman. "Well, apparently, a mob gentleman named Vincent Lambosa took offense at being invited to leave Malik's store, and attempted to blow it up...along with my people."

Flip. "Reports say that it was one of your people that saved the day."

Flip. "I understand that Patty Ferguson acted quickly and according to training, and tossed the explosive back outside the store, where it exploded."

Flip. "Joey, can you tell us what the mob was doing here, at this store?"

Flip. "Well, we had found out a few things about Mickey Giambini during the course of another investigation, so we had been looking at stopping the 'protection' payments going to him by offering our security services at no charge, for a two-week period. Of course, at the end of two weeks, we would offer those businesses that liked our services a competitive package of security."

Flip. "Mr. Malik said that your people let this mobster leave, but with a message for Mickey Giambini. What is that message, Joey?"

Flip. Joey looked at Misty, who nodded slightly. "Miriam, it relates to that other case we spoke about." Joey looked into the camera. "Mr. Giambini, let her go. Now. If you do, it all stops now. If I have to come and get her, it will cost you a *lot* more than it'll cost me. Let. Her. Go."

Flip. "Who is 'her', Joey?"

Flip. "No further comment, Miriam. Thank you for letting me say what I needed to say."

Patty stepped out of the ambulance then, supported by Brandon. Both had minor cuts on exposed skin, which had been dressed, and Patty had some bruising in places she didn't know *could* bruise, but no major harm.

Two cops that were standing near the ambulance began clapping their hands at Patty's appearance. Joey and Misty joined in. Soon, every police officer, firefighter, and ambulance attendant were all applauding Patty and Brandon.

"Applause for two heroes. Danger that intended to cause not just destruction, but death as well, averted today, thanks to two uniformed security guards from Justice Security. Miriam Apple, reporting live from the *Kwikstuff* convenience store. Back to Channel 7, where we join our original programming already in progress."

"OKAY, WE'RE OFF THE air. Joey, what's the deal with Mickey Giambini?" asked Miriam.

Joey shook his head. "I can't say anything, Miriam. I don't want it blasted all over the media."

Miriam shook her head. "Joey, Misty – this is for real. If I were going to publicize anything about Gaimbini, I would have pursued the question on the air with you. I caught myself doing that with the store owner, Malik...thank goodness I saw you, and I was able to break off his comments."

Misty looked at Miriam's face. Something she saw there made her realize that Miriam was being honest with them. Then she noticed that Steve had put down his camera and that it wasn't pointed at anything. She nudged Joey, and said, "She's telling the truth, Joey."

Miriam stared at nothing. "Yeah. The truth. It's supposed to be what a reporter reports, unless it's about someone like Giambini." She laughed. "I quit smoking a few years ago, and the only time I miss it is when I talk about Giambini, or what happened to Steve and I. About a year ago, I did a piece about Giambini's possible ties to the city's politicians, and the station actually broadcast the story. The backlash started even before the newscast went off the air. Advertisers started cancelling. Enough cancelled to cause a little bit of concern at the station...at least with the general manager. He called down to the producer of the nightly newscasts and said there were to be no more stories about Mickey Giambini on Channel 7. Then, as Steve and I were leaving for the night, a couple of thugs were waiting for us in the parking lot. They roughed Steve up a little, and one of them had a mayonnaise jar full of liquid that he said was acid, and that if we did any more stories about Mickey Giambini, he'd rearrange my looks with the acid, and they'd kill Steve." She stopped for a moment, and a tear slowly made its way down her face. "I was terrified, and I pissed myself like an excited kindergartner, but that was the night I realized something about myself. I realized that I had fallen in love with my cameraman." She wiped the tear away and stood up straight. "So, I've avoided stories about that gentleman ever since. I'm vain, and I care about my face...but I love Steve more than any of that. I don't want to lose him.

"So, Joey, you can understand...anything you want to say about Giambini is strictly and forever *off* the record," finished Miriam.

Joey shook his head. "Miriam, you really *are* human!"

Miriam slapped at Joey's arm, and smiled slightly. "Asshole."

Joey smiled, then began the story. "Yesterday, five special needs kids came to my office and wanted me to..." He told her the whole story, and left out nothing. "But, remember, Miriam – the entire thing is off the record. You can't say one word."

Miriam nodded. "Joey, I can speak for both Steve and myself when I say that we won't breathe a word, and if we can help you in some way that doesn't risk my face or his life, just let us know."

"Count on it, guys."

"SO THERE IT IS, VINCENT," said Giambini. "Your ass is saved. For today, anyway."

"What do you mean, boss?" replied Vincent, still cradling his broken elbow.

"You saw what he said, right there on the television," Giambini said. "He said, 'Let her go and it stops now.' That's just what I'm gonna do."

"Boss, she's gonna press charges! That's what you said, anyway."

"You gotta lot to learn, doncha, 'observer'? Justice is a man of his word. If he says it stops, it stops. She won't press charges, because he's gonna fix it somehow. Now, listen, you dumbass: it doesn't concern you any more. None of it. You're lucky to be walking outta here on your own power! Now get to the doc and get yourself fixed up. Forget about Jackie Blue!"

Vincent left, but he was simmering inside.

Vincent didn't care what the boss told him.

It wasn't over. Debts were owed.

And Joey Justice would pay them.

And if the boss tried to stop him...well, there were enough debts around for the boss to pay on a few, too.

PATTY AND BRANDON HAD been sent home to rest. Both had wanted to stay on, but Joey told them point blank to either go home and rest for two days, or he'd fire them. They went.

Joey and Misty walked back into the lobby of Justice Security emotionally exhausted. The couple genuinely liked the two young guards, and were relieved that their wounds were minor. However, the explosion at *Kwikstuff* emphasized Joey's resolve in hiring a medical doctor. He called Marcus Moore's cell phone.

"Marcus Moore."

"Marcus, this is Joey."

"Joey! I heard Yates jumped the garden gate with you."

"He did. He also paid the price. He needs to learn that you have to play nice to get career busts through me."

"Ayyy-men to that. How's things with the kids? Need any help with them?"

"No, but thanks anyway. Marcus, would you please have Dr. Orval Bishop give me a call at his convenience? As soon as he can?"

"Something wrong?"

"No, buddy, it's business."

"Sure, Joe. I'll call him now. He's at his office."

"Thanks, Marcus."

Joey had met Dr. Orval Eugene (*just call me Buddy*) Bishop during the Fernandez dustup a few weeks earlier, when Megan had been hit with a ricochet, and had to have fast, quiet surgery. Marcus Moore had given Joey the use of one of the FBI medical facilities in the city. Joey had taken an immediate liking to the kindly, talented doctor.

"Oh, and I'm supposed to tell you something, from a friend...let's see...how *was* that worded? Oh, yeah, and I quote: 'Let Louie do what he does best, and the boy will be fine.' Make any sense to you, Joey?"

Joey looked a bit puzzled, but he answered, "A little bit, I guess, although it's a bit cryptic. Who's the friend?"

"Cryptic is as good as it gets. And I can't tell you who the friend is, either. I told Madel...um, I mean, 'Friend' that you'd ask me that. 'Friend's' response was, and, again, I quote: 'He'll meet me soon enough.' And there you have it, my friend."

"Should I be worried, Marcus?"

Marcus was quiet for a moment. "Yes and no."

Joey chuckled. "Now *you* sound cryptic, Marcus."

"I know. 'Friend' is nothing to worry about. But if you're actually going to meet 'Friend', that situation could be...unusual, if not dangerous. I'm just not sure. Just keep your eyes open, okay?"

"Will do, Marcus. And thanks. Later."

"Later, Joey."

The two men hung up, just as Joey and Misty made it to the front desk. Tony was there.

"Bosses, somebody here that you should meet," said Tony. He gestured toward a man seated in the waiting area. Nicely dressed and well-groomed, the man stood when Joey's attention focused on him. He walked over to Joey and Misty.

"Mr. Justice, my name is Rizzo," said Rizzo. "I work for a certain gentleman that you passed a message to on the teevee a little while ago."

Misty looked at Tony, who nodded. "He's legit. He does work for Giambini."

Joey overheard as well. "So, Mr. Rizzo. I would offer to shake hands, but, under the circumstances..." He shrugged.

Rizzo smiled. "I understand completely. I would not want to shake hands with me, either, if I were in your position. Is there somewhere we can talk," he looked around, from left to right, "privately?"

Joey smiled. "Of course, sir, my office is this way." He gestured toward the elevators. Rizzo led the way.

As they walked to the elevators, Joey whispered to Misty, "Do we know anybody named...Madeline?"

Misty looked puzzled, then shook her head.

Chapter 11

Rizzo was settled in one of the soft chairs in Joey's office, holding a glass of a very expensive Irish whiskey.

"I commend you for your taste, Mr. Justice," said Rizzo.

"It was a gift from a client," replied Joey. "I have a whole case. Not to seem rude, Mr. Rizzo, but why are you here?"

Rizzo took another sip from his glass, closed his eyes, and let the liquid roll down his throat. "Absolutely heavenly." He smiled, and set the glass down on the coffee table. "On the teevee, you made an offer. You said, 'Let her go, and it stops now'. Did you mean it?"

Joey nodded once. "I did."

Rizzo smiled. "Can you guarantee that this hypothetical 'her' will not pursue recompense through the criminal justice system?"

Joey smiled. "I can't guarantee that she won't go to the cops with it, but I can strongly, emphatically encourage her to keep the last few days out of the interest of the authorities."

"I understand. That would have to do, wouldn't it? Assuming we know of who you might be speaking of, of course..."

Joey smiled again. "Of course."

"I have been authorized by Mr. Giambini to say that the situation has become...embarrassing. A fiasco from the very beginning. He wishes to be shut of the situation, preferably with no bloodshed. However, he can't be seen as 'giving in' to your declarations, which would make it extremely difficult to just...release this person. Do you understand?"

"I can see where it might cause issues in certain circumstances..."

Rizzo spread his hands. "Then you understand. But, there may be another way, if certain people are willing, and can keep their mouths shut."

"We're listening."

"One adventurous person...provided with specific directions...could go in and, um...*retrieve* a hypothetical person, and go out the way they came in.

The situation would then be resolved enough to keep everyone happy. Do you agree?"

Joey nodded slowly. "In theory, yes."

"And perhaps if it were done as quickly as...oh, *tonight,* say...everyone could achieve happiness quickly."

"Of course, one would have to have explicit directions, telling this adventurous person how to get in unobserved...with those directions, why...I believe it *could* happen as quickly as tonight, Mr. Rizzo. Hypothetically, of course."

"Of course." Rizzo reached for his drink, and a piece of paper fell out of his sport coat sleeve onto the table. Rizzo pretended not to notice. He drained his drink, looked at his now-empty glass, put it back onto the table. "Mr. Justice, I'm going to have to leave your fine company at this point in time." He stood. "I thank you for you generous hospitality, and for that taste of a delightful Irish whiskey."

Joey rose to his feet, too. "Mr. Rizzo, should this hypothetical situation resolve itself tonight, I will see to it that you, *personally,* receive a bottle from my private stock, with my compliments."

"And I thank you, sir. I look forward to hearing from you."

Joey walked with Rizzo to the office door, while Misty hung back and picked up the paper that Rizzo had dropped onto the table. The couple then escorted the mobster out of the building.

As Rizzo left, Joey turned to Tony. "Tony, please find Louie and Jessica, and have them bring the children to the situation room ASAP."

"Will do, boss."

Joey turned to Misty. "Now, let's you and I see if we can find blueprints for Giambini's building on a computer somewhere. I want to compare what Rizzo gave me with what's on file. I *don't* want to walk into a trap."

On the way to the situation room, Joey's phone rang.

"This is Joey."

"Mr. Justice, this is Dr. Bishop. Marcus Moore said you needed to talk to me. What can I help you with?"

"Dr. Bishop, thank you for getting back to me. Do you mind if I'm blunt and to the point? We sort of have a situation going here."

"Of course, Mr. Justice."

"I have been convinced that we need a medical doctor on staff here at Justice Security, and I'd like to hire you away from the FBI. I can guarantee you a very competitive salary, plus a state-of-the-art clinic-slash-hospital furnished with input from you and Dr. Caleb Mitchell, our staff psychiatrist. You will be able to also have patients within your practice that are *not* employees of Justice Security, with the codicil that our people come first. Your salary is just that: a salary. It would not be client-based or insurance-funded. Housing is available in the building, if you so desire. Dr. Mitchell keeps his own apartment outside of the Justice Security building, but housing would be included for you, should you desire. Would you be interested, Dr. Bishop?"

Joey heard silence for a few beats. "And the medical facilities would be in the Justice Security building? Built to my specifications?"

"General medicine facilities would be built to your specifications, with input from Dr. Mitchell on the psychiatric areas. You would work together when necessary, and assist each other as needed."

"Nursing staff?"

"Funding provided by the company for up to three. Anything over that would have to paid for by outside patients. What does the FBI pay you as a salary now, Doc?"

Bishop named a figure.

Joey said, "I'll double that, and consider it money well spent. What do you say, Dr. Bishop?"

There was silence for a couple of beats, then Dr. Bishop said, "When do I start?"

Joey smiled. "Now would be really nice, Doc."

LOUIE, JESSICA, MIKE Woods, and the kids all piled off of the elevator and headed down the hall toward the situation room fifteen minutes later. Jennie Lou was temporarily in a normal wheelchair – Louie had challenged the lab techs to "fancy up this girl's ride". He had told them to make it more powerful, loaded with certain extras, and easy for Jennie Lou to operate. While the lab worked their magic, Jennie Lou had to ride around in a "loaner", pushed by either Louie or Phillip. The lab promised that it wouldn't take more than six hours to "make the young lady proud".

They all chatted amongst themselves as they walked. They had spent much of the day together, and all had had a good time. Joey's summons had come just as they had finished a minor exercise program, led by Louie. Even Jessica had participated.

The chatting stopped as they walked into the situation room. Joey and Misty had several search engines functioning on the wall of screens, all searching for blueprints of the Crosselli building.

"Hi, guys!" called Joey. "Come on in – we've got news for you."

The kids all sat at the round conference table. Louie stood behind Jennie Lou, and Jessica sat between Phillip and Cynthia.

"Let me fill you all in on what's happened so far today," said Misty. She told the children everything that had happened that day, beginning with the distribution of uniformed personnel. When she got to the part about Brandon and Patty breaking Vincent's arm in *Kwikstuff*, the children cheered. When she told them the part about the explosion at the store, the children were full of concern for the two uniformed people. Misty assured them that both were okay, just bumps and bruises.

Louie quipped, "An explosion? And Joey wasn't nowhere around it?"

Jessica and Misty laughed at the remark, which referred to Joey's ability to accidentally set off almost anything explosive. Joey ignored the laughs.

Misty then told them about arriving back here to find Rizzo waiting for them, with an unusual offer...and that Joey was going to take them up on it tonight.

Mike Woods said, "Does that mean Jackie will be back tonight?"

Joey said, "I hope so, Mike. It sure looks promising."

"You hear that, kids?" said Mike. "And we just came to him yesterday morning!"

"Let's not celebrate now, okay?" said Joey. "She's not out yet."

"We're accessing blueprints for the Crosselli building right now, and we've scanned the diagram that Rizzo gave us into the computer as well," said Misty. "We'll compare them side-by-side, and make some decisions."

RIZZO REPORTED BACK to Giambini.

"Mission accomplished, boss," he told the mob boss. "I think he'll get her tonight."

"And good riddance to that piece of fluff," said Giambini. "She ain't been nuthin' but trouble since Vincent brought her here. And I ain't forgot that Lesko had a part in it, too...but since he talked the Vegas boys into giving us back our money, I'll let it slide for now." He leaned back in his desk chair, then pointed at Rizzo. "Make sure that nobody's around the building tonight that might give Justice any trouble...and make *damn* sure that there's only one lock on the bitch's door!"

"Will do, boss."

"And I want that fuckin' Vincent in here, with that fuckin' Lesko, at nine o'clock Monday morning. I gotta let 'em know that there ain't gonna be any more damn 'mystery' money."

"OKAY, SO EVERYBODY is in agreement on the way in?" asked Joey.

"Yeah, we agree on the way in," said Louie. "We *don't* agree on you goin' in by yourself."

Joey shook his head. "I know, Percival. But, Dexter isn't back until Monday, and he's the most silent of us. That leaves me."

"How is Dexter the most silent?" asked Jennie Lou.

Joey smiled. "Dexter is a martial arts expert. He learned from one of the most talented and well-known martial arts teachers in the world. Dexter could stand directly in front of you, and you wouldn't be able to see him unless he wanted you to. He's teaching all of us, but some of us have only certain talents...and none of us are as good as he is."

"I could go, Joey," said Louie.

"I know you're willing, old friend, but you don't exactly blend in to the woodwork. Neither does Jessica, or Misty. Like I said, that leaves me. I don't like going in alone, but I don't see any other option." He looked each of his partners in the eye. "Honestly, I don't think it's a trap. I really think Giambini wants us to get Jackie out of his hair. I think he became engrossed in visions of sugar plums, and Jackie either couldn't, or wasn't willing to deliver."

"Hey, what about this guy 'Vincent'?" said Mike Woods. "Do you think he's anything to worry about?"

"Well, he *does* have reason not to like us," said Jessica. "First Phillip almost chokes him to death, then Brandon and Patty break his elbow. I don't think I'd count him as a friend to the company."

"Me, either," said Joey. "We'll just have to hope that Giambini has a big enough hold on him to keep him quiet."

"Yeah," said Louie. He slapped Phillip on the back as he said, "I'd hate to have to turn my man Phillip loose on him again!"

AT TEN O'CLOCK THAT night, a tallish, nondescript man wearing camouflage pants, a black t-shirt, black baseball hat with no logo, and dark hiking boots picked the lock on door number twelve on the loading dock of the Crosselli building. He entered quickly and unseen, debated locking the door behind him, and finally left it pushed closed but unlocked. He carried a full-sized Maglite flashlight with the lens covered with black felt. There was a small hole in the felt that allowed a pencil of light to escape, illuminating only what crossed the thin beam's path.

Joey briefly consulted the piece of paper that Rizzo had provided, then shined the light ahead of him. Sure enough, there was the shipping office. According to the diagram, the stairs he needed were to the immediate right of the the dark office. Joey started walking slowly, passing parked forklifts and full cardboard boxes as he went. When he came to the office, he turned right. Ten steps in front of him was the stairwell.

Even though the building appeared deserted, Joey knew it wasn't. Misty had dropped him off at the mouth of the alley leading to the loading docks, but he had used a device that picked up infrared heat signatures within the building. There were approximately thirty different heat signatures that were identified as human within the building, but it looked as if none of them were on his diagrammed path. This was confirmation, at least in *his* mind, that Giambini really meant for them to take Jackie out of their hair.

However, crossing the ten steps with no cover was very, very difficult for Joey. He crossed the open space, however, with no harm done, and he very gently opened the door to the stairwell. The door threw a crack of light across the deserted loading dock's staging area, and Joey quickly ducked into the stairwell and pressed himself against the wall. He heard nothing, and actually jumped when the door latched.

Rizzo's diagram said that the holding cell was on the fourth floor. Joey slowly started climbing the stairs.

BACK AT THE JUSTICE Security building, Louie, Jessica, Mike Woods, and the children were all gathered in the situation room, watching a state-of-the-art video feed on one of the flat-panel, high definition monitors on the wall. The feed consisted of a computer-generated layout of the floor plan of the Crosselli building, and, imposed on the stairwell's image, was a man-shaped avatar representing Joey, who was wearing a tracking device while inside the building.

The children laughed when they caught Louie "helping" the avatar tiptoe up the stairs by doing the same.

MISTY WAS PARKED DOWN the block from the Crosselli building, watching the avatar's progress on a small, hand-held screen. Her heart was pounding with worry.

JOEY HAD REACHED THE door opening into the fourth floor. He grasped the knob and gently turned it. When it turned as far as it would turn, he opened the door a slight bit, just a tiny crack. He put one eye to the crack, and found himself peering down a long hallway. Within his small vantage point, he could see the door that his diagram had indicated.

A door with three sturdy bolts, two of which were open.

Jacqueline Belew was behind that door, if Rizzo could be believed.

Okay, so far, so good. Rizzo told the truth. So, do I just walk over to the door and throw the bolt back? It's only five steps, and I haven't run up on anybody yet. Rizzo said that the way would be easy. Oh, well, why the hell not?

Joey opened the door normally and strode boldly over to the door, threw the bolt, opened the door, and entered the room. He pushed the door closed behind him.

Sitting on the cot, blinking sleep and surprise from her eyes, sat an attractive lady.

"Jackie Blue, I presume?" asked Joey with a half-smile. "I'm Joey Justice. You ready to get out of here?"

Jackie's mouth opened with an "O" of surprise, then she leapt from the cot and threw her arms around Joey with a huge bear hug. Tears began flowing while she said, "Oh, thank God!" over and over.

Joey was a bit surprised by her reaction. He finally hugged the crying woman back, and said, "Jackie, we have to go. I trust these people, but only for certain things, and only for a short while."

Jackie looked up into his eyes. "What do you mean?"

Joey shook his head. "Not now. Not until we're far from here."

"Please. How are the children?"

Joey smiled. "They're great. They've made themselves quite at home at the Justice Security building. They're waiting for us now."

Jackie nodded. "I'm right behind you, Mr. Justice."

"The name's Joey. Mr. Justice is my dad," Joey replied. He cracked the door open, looked both ways, and gestured for Jackie to follow him. They walked the five steps over to the stairwell, opened the door, then began the trip down four flights.

"HE'S ON HIS WAY DOWN!" said Cynthia excitedly.

"Does that mean he's found Jackie?" asked Nicky.

"I sure hope it does, kids," said Mike Woods.

They continued to watch the avatar's progress.

WHEN JOEY REACHED THE bottom of the stairs, he opened the door to the staging area, turned to Jackie, and pressed his index finger against his lips. Jackie nodded.

The pair tiptoed through the darkness, passing beside forklifts and cardboard boxes, until they reached the door that Joey had opened earlier. They went out the door, onto the loading dock. Then, they were walking briskly but casually along the alley.

At the opening, Misty screeched to a halt just as Joey and Jackie arrived. Joey opened a car door for Jackie, then he climbed into the car himself, as Misty took off.

"Jacqueline Belew, I'd like you to meet my fiance, Misty Wilhite," said Joey.

Misty caught Jackie's eyes in the rear view mirror and smiled at the foster mom. "Hi, Jackie. I've certainly heard a lot about you the last couple of days."

Jackie shook her head. "This is happening so fast! Did the children actually come to you?"

Joey nodded. "They came yesterday morning, along with Mike Woods. We'll fill you in on all of it once we get to the building, okay?"

Jackie nodded. "Whatever you think is best, Joey."

WHEN THEY ARRIVED AT the Justice Security building, they parked on the street in front of the entrance. They walked into the lobby, and were greeted by Jimmy Brooks, the night man.

"Hello, Miss Belew," said Jimmy. "Glad to see you safe and sound. I know the children will be relieved."

Jackie, taken by surprise that a uniformed front desk man would know who she was, simply said, "Thank you."

Misty said, "In a case like yours, everyone at Justice Security knows who you are, and what's happening with the case at any time. It helps more than it hurts, because often a tip comes from someone that noticed something small...and it could solve a pending case."

Jackie nodded. "I see."

Entering the elevator, Joey pressed the button for the fourth floor. "The children are with our partners, Louie Washington and Jessica Queen, in the situation room. Dexter Beck and his new wife Megan are still on their honeymoon, and won't be back until Monday. Mike Woods is with them, and has been a big help during this time. I believe he stayed with the children and took care of them until they all came here." The elevator opened on four, and Joey led the way to the situation room.

As he walked in, he said, "Anybody here looking for Jackie Blue?"

Every head in the room turned and looked at Joey, then looked behind him, at Jackie.

Jackie waved and said, "Hey! Anybody miss me?"

The three closest children were Nicky, Cynthia, and Tommy. They got to Jackie first, and practically pounced on her. Phillip began smiling, and pushed Jennie Lou over to Jackie, who hugged each child with a lengthy hug, even Phillip. Phillip was enough in the moment that he was able to bear hug Jackie.

Then, Jackie caught sight of Mike Woods, who had stood quietly and let the children have their moment. Jackie moaned, and threw herself into the big man's arms. After a quiet moment, she looked up at him and kissed him.

While the couple was kissing, the kids all smiled at each other. Joey and Misty found each other's hands and held them. Louie and Jessica smiled as they saw the smiles on the children's faces.

Finally, the kiss broke. Jackie looked at Mike, then at the children. "I'm sorry I got you all into this. I'd understand if none of you wanted anything to do with me anymore."

The kids looked at each other silently, not knowing what to say...until Cynthia summed it up for them.

"Jackie, you're our mom," she said simply.

"Yeah," said Tommy. "We love you."

And that was the end of that path of the conversation.

"I think it's time to fill you in on everything that's happened since you were taken," said Joey. "I'll let the kids tell their part, then I'll take over once they get to the part about coming here."

And the kids *did* tell her. They told her how scared they were. They told her that they remembered what she told them, and that they almost called the police anyway.

"Good thing you didn't," interrupted Louie. "Half the cops in this town are on Giambini's payroll."

They told her about Mike Woods, and how he stayed with them until Friday morning, and how he brought them to Justice Security. They told her about meeting Tony Armstrong and Misty in the lobby, and how Misty and Turk put them in Joey's office.

"Oooo, and wait until you see Joey's office, Jackie," said Jennie Lou. "It's soooo nice!"

Jackie smiled and said, "Jennie Lou, where is your wheelchair?"

Joey smiled at her and said, "That's where we come in, I'm afraid..."

"I got the lab workin' on some things on Jen's chair," said Louie. "You ain't even gonna recognize it when they get through!"

Jackie said, "Mr. Justice, I can't afford all that...I probably can't afford to pay you for rescuing me."

Joey held up a hand. "Believe me, it's my pleasure...and my responsibility."

Jackie looked puzzled. "Responsibility?"

"Let's start from the top," he replied. "When I met the children and Mike, I accepted a few things at face value. I accepted that they were telling the truth, I accepted that you have a gift, and I accepted that Mickey Giambini wanted that gift to make money. I gathered from the children's story that you knew that Louie would win the fight, but you didn't know that he would resign the win because he delayed the fight, and that it would never be an honest win to a man of integrity...like our Louie." He gestured to his friend, who ran his hand over his bald head as if it was a full head of hair. "I gathered through some things that the children said that you overheard that Giambini was the one that provided the explosive material used by Esteban Fernandez to try to blow up the convention center. Because of *that* fact, I wanted Giambini. Bad. So, I had to talk to my partners, and they said..."

Joey finished the story.

The room was quiet while Jackie processed everything that had been done to rescue her.

Joey broke the silence. "So, you understand why it's my responsibility?"

"Not every man would go to such lengths to have himself appointed guardian of a group of kids, much less a group of *special needs* kids," Jackie replied.

Joey shook his head. "Number one: The only special need these kids have is that they want to know somebody in their lives cares about them. Number two: I'm not the only man that would have done that." He nodded in Mike Woods's direction. "I'm just the one that could."

Mike stood tall. "He's right, Jackie. I'd adopt every one of them, if they'd have me for a father."

Jackie looked puzzled. "But, Mr. Justice...you didn't get your man."

Joey shook his head. "It's okay, Jackie. Getting you back safely, and being assured that I wasn't going to be risking my two best uniforms again, made it worth waiting for another time. I'll have my revenge against Giambini one day...just not today."

Jessica said, "You must be tired, Jackie. Would you like to bunk with the girls, or would you prefer...*other* arrangements?"

Jackie glanced at Mike, with a small smile. "I think it would be best if I bunk with the girls. Thank you."

Joey stood. "Well, in that case...I suggest we all turn in. If you folks would like to join us for breakfast, we can meet at nine-thirty in the cafeteria. After breakfast, we'll give you the grand tour of Justice Security. And I'd like to have a doctor check you out, Jackie, just to be on the safe side. You'll like him – his name is Dr. Bishop, and he loves kids."

AFTER JACKIE SAID GOOD night to Mike Woods, Jessica showed Jackie to the room that she'd be sharing with the girls.

"Oh, my *God!*" said Jackie, when she saw the size of the room. "When you said 'bunking with the girls', I imagined all three of us crammed into one king-sized bed! I had no idea!"

Jessica smiled. "The girls can show you the room, and how to call out if you need anything. I live down the hall. See you girls for breakfast!" She waved and left.

Jackie began helping the girls get ready for bed.

IN THE LOBBY, THE STREET doors opened, and a man and a woman entered the building. Both were wearing large *sombreros* and *serapes*. They stopped just inside the doors, embraced, and kissed passionately.

The uniformed guard at the door, Jim Crowe, was new to Justice Security. Tall, think, and in his early fifties, he had just started working within the last week, and was full of himself. After smirking at the couple, thinking they were drunk, he moved forward. The man at the desk, Mark Haase, the night man, started to stop Crowe, then decided that discretion was the better part of valor. Also, he didn't like the Crowe.

"Excuse me, sir, ma'am," said Crowe, as he reached for the man's shoulder. The man grabbed Crowe's hand and flipped him so that Crowe landed on his back on the floor, then the man followed through with his feet on Crowe's windpipe. The woman, meanwhile, had produced twin Glock semi-automatics and had them pointed, side by side, at Crowe's eyeballs.

"Is he okay, Mark?" asked the man.

Mark Haase was laughing quietly. He regained his composure somewhat in order to answer the question. "I can't vouch for 'okay', Mr. Beck, but he *does* work for us."

The woman tucked the Glocks back under her *serape*, and the man removed his foot from Crowe's windpipe and offered a hand up to the man. He took it, and stood.

"Lesson number one from me, man," said the man called Beck. "Keep your distance from people until you ascertain identities and what business concerns them." He held out his hand to shake. "Dexter Beck. I'm one of the partners here, and this is my wife, Megan. We live here."

Megan said, "A pleasure, sir. Do you have a name, or is it just 'man'?"

Crowe, nonplussed, said, "Jim Crowe. I just started this week."

"Well, Mr. Crowe, let me say this," said Dexter. "I teach martial arts to all of our new people. Since Megan and I have been on our honeymoon, you and I haven't had the pleasure." He looked into Crowe's eyes. "But, I *will* have the pleasure – Monday morning, seven AM, in the gym. And prepare yourself, because I *will* dump you on your ass. Repeatedly." He turned to the reception desk. As he approached, he stopped and bowed to Mark. "Good evening, Mr. Haase. I certainly hope you're doing well."

Haase started chuckling at Dexter. "Doing fine now, Mr. Beck. It was a pleasure seeing that snooty prick get tail feathers pulled a little bit."

"Snooty?" asked Megan. "What is there to be snooty about?"

"I'm not sure, Megan. But one thing about our friend Crowe – if he thinks he can buffalo you, or if he remotely thinks that his station in life may be a bit higher than yours, he'll certainly lord it over you," answered Haase.

Dexter said, *sotto voce*, "Is that why you didn't try to stop him?"

Haase looked into Dexter's eyes directly. "Yes, it is. I wanted to see him brought down a couple of pegs."

Dexter nodded. "Understood. I'll dump him many, many times Monday, just for you."

Haase nodded. "Thank you, sir. I would greatly appreciate it."

Megan said, "Can I dump him a couple of times, sweet husband?"

"Of course you can," said Dexter. He turned again to Mark Haase. "Anything going on, Mark?"

Haase nodded. "Something happening, and it has to do with Mickey Giambini. We were looking for a lost lady, but we found her tonight, so I don't know if the Giambini thing is still going or not."

Dexter nodded. He had not kept in touch while on his honeymoon, so he wasn't aware of the Giambini situation.

"Who's been running it?" asked Dexter, meaning which partner was in charge.

"Looks like Mr. Justice had this one, sir. You might want to let him know you're back, and ask him to fill you in."

Dexter waved his hand as if brushing the idea away. "Joey is quite capable, Mark. He doesn't need me gumming up the works."

Haase smiled. "Yes, sir." A light began flashing on one of Haase's consoles. "Hmmm...stairwell door on six just opened."

"One of the partners, probably," said Megan.

Haase studied the console. There were no security cameras on the sixth floor, because the partners didn't want their living quarters spied on. However, each door was fixed with an indicator that showed if it was open or not. Haase shook his head. "I don't think so, sir. Mr. Washington has retired for the night, and so have Mr. Justice and Miss Wilhite."

Dexter's eyes perked up.

Megan said, "C'mon, Dexter, let's go kick their asses into next week!"

"Hold on, honey...let's see what their objective is first."

Another light began flashing on the console. Haase said, "Apparently, you're the objective, sir. The door to your apartment just opened and closed."

"Sound the alarm for the partners, Mark – tell them it's my place."

"Yes, sir."

"WOULD YOU LOOK AT THE coolness in this place?" said Nicky, pointing to a collection of swords displayed on one wall of the main room.

"They're pretty neat, Nicky, but we don't need to be here," said Tommy. "We already got in trouble for that stunt with the bathrooms. I don't want to get in trouble for this, too, and Jackie will think up an even *worse* punishment."

"Reeee-lax, would you? Nobody knows we're here, Tommy! Everybody's asleep."

They advanced further into the room. Dexter's main room was sparsely furnished, but contained several weapon displays, and a definite Oriental motif. Standing guard was an authentic early Chinese suit of armor.

"Wow," said Nicky quietly. "I wonder how old *this* is?"

"Fifth century B.C., made entirely of bronze, and it's priceless," came a voice from behind them.

Nicky and Tommy jumped as far as their leg braces would let them, then whirled around. Standing behind them was Jessica Queen, Joey Justice, Louie Washington, Misty Wilhite (who looked extremely *hot* in her shortie nightgown, thought Nicky), and two people that the boys didn't know.

"You know, boys, if you'd wanted a tour of our apartment, all you had to do was ask," said Megan. "I'm Megan Beck, and this is my husband, Dexter. That's *his* Chinese suit of armor you were about to touch."

"Can you two comprehend the amount of trouble you're in?" said Joey. "Breaking and entering is just the *least* of it!"

Louie began speaking quietly into a hand-held radio.

"We're sorry," said Nicky.

"You were 'sorry' with the bathroom stunt!" said Joey. "This goes wayyyyy beyond sorry!"

"Easy, Joey!" said Dexter. "No harm done, okay? Who *are* these kids, anyway?"

"Our clients," replied Misty, with a smile. "A bit more for Joey."

Dexter looked at Megan, then back at his partners. "Huh? What am I missing?"

"Joey's their foster dad," said Misty, still smiling.

Jackie Blue, summoned by Louie, came into the apartment, struggling with the two ends of the robe tie. "What is going on? Where is this?" She saw the two boys. "*What* have you two done now?"

Megan said, "Okay, so who is *this?*" as she pointed a thumb toward Jackie.

"That's their foster *mom*," said Misty, about to break out laughing.

Mike Woods came in, pushing Jennie Lou in her loaner wheelchair. He was followed by Phillip and Cynthia.

"Okay, so who are these people?" asked Dexter.

"More of Joey's foster kids, and the fiance of the their foster mom," said Misty, who couldn't hold it back any longer. She began laughing at the situation.

"Sure, come on in, make yourselves at home," said Megan sarcastically.

Turk, also summoned by Louie from his apartment on the fifth floor, came into the apartment, followed by Mark Haase.

"So, we found the mice in the machine, did we?" asked Haase.

"Not them two again," said Turk with a groan.

"*HOLD IT!*" shouted Dexter. Everyone turned to look at him.

"Who are all these people, why are they in our home, and what in the name of God is going on?"

Misty started giggling again, and so did Jessica. Cynthia started to laugh when Jessica did, and that made Jennie Lou laugh. Soon, everyone was laughing.

Everyone except Dexter and Megan.

"Okay," said Joey, waving his arms. "Okay. Mark, you and Turk take the children downstairs. Turk, you are to do whatever it takes to keep those two little hoodlums from getting out again – sit on them if you have to. Mark, you help him. Dexter, if you and Megan will extend your hospitality for a bit longer for everyone that remains, we'll try to explain."

Chapter 12

Sunday breakfast in the cafeteria at nine-thirty the next morning was a laid-back, good-natured affair, with everyone in attendance. It was a good relaxing way for Jackie to get used to being free again, and to see the interaction between the children and the Justice Security people. Turk came, and was actually seen smiling at Nicky and Tommy. He denied it, of course.

"Ain't smilin' at those two," he said when confronted. "I don't smile at hoodlums." He gave the two boys his best scowl, then stuffed a whole biscuit into his mouth when no one *but* the boys could see.

After most had completed eating, Joey tapped his spoon on his glass for attention.

"Folks," he said. "I hope you've enjoyed this breakfast, and this time together. This is kind of a celebration, not just for Jackie and Mike and the kids, but for us as well. We'd like to welcome our poor lost honeymooned friends and partners, Dexter and Megan Beck, back home. We love both of them, and wish them all the happiness in the world with each other." He raised his glass of white grape juice, and everyone else followed suit. "A toast to all of us: Let us never forget what love and devotion can do."

Murmurs of "hear, hear" and "you got that right" could be heard as everyone took a drink.

Joey resumed speaking. "Now, something different. Yesterday, my friend Louie Washington promised something special to a certain young lady. The lab took over, with promises that providing that something special wouldn't take more than a few hours. Well, they missed the target on that one – it's taken almost twenty-four. But, without further delay, here's Randy Brown from the lab, with Jennie Lou's new wheelchair!"

Everyone applauded as the wheelchair was wheeled into the cafeteria. It was black and chrome. The chair itself was several inches higher than a normal wheelchair, and the area under the seat was completely enclosed. The seat was made of sturdy memory foam, designed for maximum comfort for many hours of sitting. The back gave support, also utilizing memory foam, and was not as wide as a regular wheelchair. The top of the back, along with the handles, was raked backwards, to give a pleasant illusion of speed. The footrests were bigger and thicker than normally seen in a wheelchair, and an operations pad was placed on the right side, with a joystick control. Beside the headrest was another operations panel, utilizing a straw...that is, it could be controlled by breathing into the straw. The armrests were wide, and used soft foam to keep the user's arms comfortable.

Jennie Lou broke into tears at the sight of the chair, and so did Jackie.

Joey moved over to the side of the chair. "Louie, if you would please assist Miss Gwin into her new transportation?"

Louie picked Jennie Lou up and gently placed her in the new wheelchair. He then kissed the top of her head, and said, "It ain't walkin', honey, but it sure does make not walkin' comfortable."

Joey walked over to her, pointed to the lab tech, and said, "Jen, this is Randy Brown. He'll show you what's new about this chair, and all the little surprises that we installed."

Jennie Lou looked at Joey with tears in her eyes. "Thank you. I just...*thank* you."

Joey waved it off, fighting back tears of his own. "Nothing to it, sweet girl. Nothing to thank me for."

Everyone had stood to see the new wheelchair, Jacqueline Belew among them. When she saw it, and the kind, patient way Randy Brown had of showing her the proper operation of the chair, she walked over to Joey, who had retreated to Misty's side.

"I have only one thing to say to you, sir," said Jackie. She put out her hand, and, mustering all of her dignity, said, "Thank you, from the bottom of my heart."

"It's for Jen," said Joey.

"My Joey loves those kids very much, Jackie," said Misty.

Jackie nodded her agreement. Just then, from behind her, Jennie Lou squealed.

"It's *heated!* Can you believe it? The seat is *heated!*"

Everyone laughed, then applauded. Jennie Lou blushed.

DR. ORVAL EUGENE BISHOP smiled at Jackie. "Please call me 'Buddy'. Joey has asked me to examine the children thoroughly and ascertain whether further examination by specialists would be of help."

"But, Doctor...I mean, Buddy...I can't afford any doctors outside of the network that the state provides. Unless you take the insurance given to the children as wards of the state..."

Buddy laughed. "Joey didn't tell you?"

Jackie looked puzzled. "Tell me what, Buddy?"

"That all of this is absolutely no cost to you. The company is picking up the tab. And that I'm on the Justice Security staff, so my fees are nonexistent."

"Oh, my. I can't let him do all this! It's too much!"

Buddy held up a hand. "Wait a minute, Jackie, hold up! You're also forgetting something: Joey is their foster parent, too. And he has money through this company. And his partners are also fully supporting his choice to become foster parent to these children. No expense will be spared for their total health care...compliments of their foster father."

Jackie closed her mouth and shook her head. She *had* forgotten that Joey was their foster father. Well, the gift of chance never showed her *this!*

"You're right, of course, Doctor...I mean, Buddy," she replied. "I'm very grateful to him for all of this."

"One last thing, Miss Belew, then we'll get started with the children. Miss Wilhite told me today the amount donated to St. Jude Children's Hospital in Memphis by this company every year." He named the figure, which was *very* high. "Apparently, Joey also does a few other undercover things to benefit children every year. I say all that to say this: St. Jude is one of my personal blessings, and because of that, I'm very, very *proud* to provide health care for this company. When Joey does it, Joey *means* it." He reached for a file. "Let's start with little Miss Cynthia and her diagnosis of cerebral palsy, shall we? And I apologize for the crudity of the equipment today – I'm using Dr. Caleb Mitchell's psychiatric tools because we haven't had time to set up my clinic yet."

LATER, DR. BISHOP, Jackie, Misty, Mike Woods, and Joey were seated in Joey's office. Everyone had drinks, made by Joey. It was four o'clock Sunday afternoon.

"Okay," said Dr. Bishop. "That is *good* Irish whiskey!"

Joey laughed. "That reminds me – I owe a bottle of that to Rizzo."

"Well," said Dr. Bishop. "Okay, back to business. Joey, let's start with the bad news, shall we? Cynthia's diagnosis of CP is right on the money. There's nothing that can be done for her right now, although research into the disease continues. I wish I could offer more to hope for, but that's all I can say. It's a heartbreaking disease, and I'd love to see it become extinct.

"Speaking of extinct diseases, Nicky had one, and at an early age. Polio should be eradicated by now, but it still pops up here and there, especially if you've never been vaccinated. Nicky hadn't. His legs have about forty percent usage, and that's all he'll *ever* have. If he had only had the vaccine – hell, most health departments offer it for free!"

Dr. Bishop shook his head in disgust. "So, there's nothing that can be done for little Nicky, either." He took a sip of his drink, then smiled. "Now, on to Tommy. His spine was almost severed by his father's suicidal rampage, but...the doctors were able to gently push it back into place, put the boy into a back brace, and to hope for the best." He took another sip. "Whatever they did, it worked. Tommy can walk now without the leg braces. His muscles need to be built back up, but a nominal exercise regimen can do that. Tommy is almost cured...physically. Mentally, and this is probably something for Dr. Mitchell to explore, he needs work."

"I'll have Caleb begin with him immediately," said Joey.

"I'd like to discuss Jennie Lou now," said Dr. Bishop firmly. He stood, and walked to the small bar. "Anyone else ready?" There were no takers. The doctor poured himself a couple more inches of Irish whiskey. "Please forgive me. I was hesitant to discuss it before, and I still am."

Jackie asked tentatively, "What's wrong with my Jen, Dr. Bishop?"

The doctor smiled, almost to himself. He shook his head while he did, and said, "Nothing's wrong...it's what may be *right* that has me concerned."

"What do you mean, Buddy?" asked Joey.

Dr. Bishop took a breath. "After the accident that crippled Jennie Lou, apparently doctors from the ER put her back together, but it appears that they did so with no expectation that she would live to see any results. By the time they figured out that she *would* live, it was too late to go back and fix what they pieced together. When I examined her, I ran my hand along her spinal cord. I felt a bump, and I then looked at the bump I'd found. On her spine is a raised bump where the bone is jutting out a little bit."

"I've seen that bump!" exclaimed Jackie.

Buddy nodded. "Then you know what I'm talking about. I decided that I needed an X-ray, but I was stymied by the fact that I don't have one here yet. And I remember Marcus Moore talking about..."

"Tony's package machine!" said Misty. Buddy nodded.

Joey explained. "Our lead grunt has an X-ray machine downstairs in the room behind the reception desk. It has a conveyor belt, and he uses it to scan packages. Only, I think Dr. Bishop used it for Jennie Lou."

"I did, and I actually was able to get a screen capture good enough to show you what I need to." He raised a printout. "I had to ask Dexter to assist me with printing it out, and it came through wonderfully."

On the paper, a perfect X-ray of Jennie Lou's back ribs and spinal cord could be seen. He had put Jennie on her stomach to go through the machine, and the bump was displayed prominently. It looked as if the vertebrae had been put together, but not accurately. It was off by a fraction of an inch, and had healed off center.

"By healing off center the way that it did, the spinal cord wasn't given an opportunity to heal completely...just portions of the nerves in the cord were able to repair themselves. The others remained severed, causing Jen to be almost quadriplegic." He took a big gulp of his drink. "I believe that with the assistance of a top-notch surgeon, a lot of physical therapy, and lots of love and support by people that care about her...I believe Jennie Lou can be almost normal again."

Mike Woods spoke up. "You mean she'll be able to walk again?"

"Walk, dance, recite poetry, smart off to her caregivers...have a normal life. If I'm correct with my diagnosis, and it's just a preliminary diagnosis, I believe it can happen. And, if Joey is okay with it, I know a fantastic surgeon from St. Jude that could perform the surgery, if the company will take care of his expenses and arrange a quality operating theater."

The room was silent.

"You really believe she can be...fixed?" asked Jackie, with awe in her voice.

"I believe so...but, of course, the chance exists that I'm totally wrong. That's why I was hesitant to talk about her. I didn't want to raise hopes that could be false. I mean, we'll definitely want a second opinion."

"Then, make the arrangements," said Joey. "Today, if you can...tomorrow without fail. If we need to send Jennie to St. Jude, we'll do that as well. I think Louie would welcome the chance to be that child's bodyguard!"

Everyone smiled. Then, a quiet question came from Jackie.

"And what about Phillip?"

Dr. Bishop looked at Jackie above the rim of his glass, then brought it down. After a moment, he began speaking.

"Autism is easy to diagnose, but difficult to put into a convenient defined box. Jackie, did you ever read Phillip's case file? His court file, and why he wound up in your care?"

Jackie shook her head. "No. The juvenile judge in that case ordered the file closed."

Dr. Bishop nodded. "I read it. It's one of the benefits of being a former doctor with the FBI that works for one of the world's premier computer hackers. Dexter assisted me with it." He took a last sip from his glass and gently placed it on the table. "Let me say this before I go any further: Autism can be caused by epileptic seizures. Epileptic seizures can be caused by blunt trauma to the head, causing brain injury. According to the evidence in the court file, Phillip's mother died during childbirth, leaving him to be raised by his father. In the first grade, Phillip was admitted to the emergency room. He had epileptic seizures. But, that wasn't the reason he was admitted. His six-year-old bruised and battered body was found lying in his front yard, where he had crawled after being beaten senseless by his alcoholic father, trying to 'get the Devil out of the boy so he'd stop pitching fits'. The head trauma he received in the beating apparently stopped the seizures, but brought on a mild case of autism." He paused. "There isn't a cure. He's avoided slipping deeper into the autism by Jackie's attentions, and by his connection to Jennie Lou. He could go deeper, but it isn't likely."

Everyone was quiet for a moment. Then, Joey rose from the padded chair and walked to his desk. He pressed the button for the building-wide announcement system, and said, "Louie, please bring Jennie Lou to my office as soon as you can. Louie, please bring Jennie Lou to my office as soon as you can. Thanks."

He looked around the room. "I'd say that it's time to tell the girl, wouldn't you?"

JENNIE LOU'S REACTION went from wide-eyed excitement to narrow-eyed suspicion.

"You aren't teasing me, are you?" she asked, eyeing Dr. Bishop.

Joey knelt beside her. "Sweetheart, if it were teasing, I wouldn't be here."

"So I could really walk again?"

"The possibility exists, Jennie," replied Dr. Bishop. "Your back would have to be broken again, then micro-surgery to repair the nerves in the spinal cord, then a body cast, back brace, lots of therapy, and lots of prayers...but, yes, I believe you can walk again."

Jennie Lou sat still for a moment, looking down at her useless left arm, her partially useful right arm, and her limp legs. When she looked up, there were tears in her eyes. "Do you know how much I've prayed and hoped for this?"

Everyone in the room took a turn holding her while she cried.

LATER, JACKIE FOUND the partners.

"Mike and I have been talking," she said. "We're going home in the morning, and we'd like to invite all six of you, and Turk, and Dr. Bishop to go with us. We want to have a big sitdown dinner with you folks. It's the least we can do for everything you've done for us."

"Yeah, we could sit around in the yard, play with the kids," said Mike. "And we know the kids would love to have you!"

Misty spoke up. "You know, it's time that the Justice Security partners took a weekday off. We can leave Tony Armstrong in charge. Joey and I will be there."

Dexter said, "Megan and I were both wishing for one more day to adjust to being home. We'll be there!"

Louie said, "Just *try* keeping me away."

"I'll be there, too," said Jessica. "What can we bring?"

Chapter 13

The big front yard at Jackie's house on Peach Street was full that Monday afternoon.

Joey and Misty had earlier had some grunts pick up some picnic and outdoor items, and deliver and assemble them at Jackie's house. Included in the purchases was a picnic table, a huge charcoal grill, several comfortable outdoor chairs, three small outdoor tables, and a large, open tent to cover the picnic table. The tent had zippered mesh doors that kept out the insects while still allowing a breeze to flow through.

Along with the lawn furniture, bundles of colorful helium balloons had been attached, both to the tent and to the picnic table. A huge, real-wood insulated barrel had been filled with ice and various sodas, juices, and bottles of water...it had been decided that since this was a family get-together of sorts, that alcohol would not be appropriate. Streamers had been hung here and there, and fluttered in the wind. The sun was shining brightly, and the temperature was in the low eighties. Everyone thought it was a beautiful day.

The adults were broken off into groups of two or three, and the five children were scattered around the yard among the groups. At the picnic were the six partners from Justice Security, Jacqueline Belew and Mike Woods, Dr. Bishop, and Turk. Coming along for the ride were Brandon King and Patty Ferguson, and Charlie Li. Charlie was one of the members of both Dexter and Jessica's core teams. Charlie, Dexter, and Joey were explaining to Mike Woods how they had pissed off Esteban Fernandez beyond the point of no return, and made a mortal enemy of the man. Misty and Jessica were attending to the hamburgers and hot dogs on the grill. Cynthia was seated near them, smiling contentedly while Megan chatted with both her and the two older women. Louie and Turk had the boys out in the yard, teaching them various upper body exercises. Jackie was inside the house with Dr. Bishop, paying close attention as Brandon and Patty explained how Phillip saved all of their lives on Friday by coming up behind Vincent. Jennie Lou, having discovered that her new wheelchair had a double bank of batteries and a longer run time, was on the front porch. She was flying back and forth on the porch, trying to see how long it would take to run her batteries down. As far as Jennie Lou was concerned, it was a good day.

In short, everyone was enjoying the day and the company. It was a *good* day.

VINCENT WAS DOWN THE street, hiding and watching from Mrs. Morgan's house again. He had gained entry by breaking the "crime scene do not cross" tape across the back door, picking the lock, and making himself at home.

He didn't feel bad about it, because he and Mrs. Morgan had been quite intimate just a few weeks earlier.

After the Giambini doctor had fixed up his arm on Saturday, Vincent had only one thing on his mind: blowing the life away out of Jacqueline Belew.

Vincent didn't much care what Mickey Giambini said about her...or about Joey Justice. It wasn't over. Not until he had some payback.

He knew that Jackie would come home eventually, so he had taken up residence here. Today, the gamble had paid off. Then, as he observed, members of Justice Security kept showing up. Vincent had to alter his original plan, from silently entering the house and killing the bitch and the crips and the retards, to waiting to try to take out all of them at once.

Yep, thought Vincent. *It's a* good *day!*

JOEY WAS HAVING A GREAT time. It had been a long while since he and Misty had just had fun, with no case staring them in the face.

As for cases, this one was just about wrapped up. They had found Jackie Blue, which was what the children had hired them to do. The confrontation with Mickey Giambini, which they had all expected to happen violently well before now, became a non-event, with each of them going their separate ways. Perhaps one day they'd clash again, but, for now, they'd leave each other alone. *And that's a good thing,* he thought to himself. *We only need one dangerous, egotistical madman after us at a time, and Fernandez still ranks as number one...*

Earlier, Jackie had approached Joey about a fee.

"Jackie," he told her, "I don't know if you have a gift or not. I haven't seen it happen firsthand. If you do, here's what you need to do for my fee: buy a major lottery ticket, like Powerball or something, and put the winning numbers on it. That's my fee. Otherwise, forget about it, okay?"

A few minutes later, Mike Woods had left to pick up more soda and chips. When he returned, Jackie again came to Joey.

"Here it is, Joey, with my thanks for all you've done," she told him, and handed him a lottery ticket with one Powerball number across it.

Joey took it, smiled, and put it into his wallet. "Good. And when it wins, Jackie, we'll split the jackpot, and use the money to set up the kids for the rest of their lives. How's that?"

Jackie smiled back at Joey. "It's a deal, foster dad!"

Now, Joey watched the interaction between all of the people that had become close in such a short period of time, and was grateful. It was a good day.

Misty called out, "Okay, people, soup's on! Let's eat!"

That was when Hell came to the picnic.

VINCENT HAD OBSERVED his targets until he guessed that most of them were in the front yard. He took his leave of the Morgan house by way of the back door. He had stolen a "beater" car – an old late eighties two-door Caddy - just in case some of the neighbors happened to be out. He didn't want anyone to be able to identify his car.

He also faced another problem with what he was going to do...he only had one arm. The other was secured in a metal brace that kept it at a ninety-degree angle. He had to drive with that arm, so that limited what he was able to do. No grenades or explosives could be thrown. So, he was left with firearms.

Vincent finally chose to use his Uzi automatic. Easy to hold, no aim required, and, best of all, a fifty round magazine of 9mm metal death.

It was a *really* good day.

NICKY WAS THE ONE THAT saw the car approaching at five miles per hour. He thought it was odd that a car would be going so slow, even through a neighborhood. Then he saw the gun poking its ugly nose through the car's window.

The next few seconds seemed as if they happened in slow motion.

"GUN!" shouted Nicky. He turned to run and immediately became tangled in his leg braces. He fell to the ground, bumping into Tommy, who got tangled in his own leg braces and also fell to the ground.

Turk was the closest to the two boys. He spotted the gun as it began to fire, and dove to shield the boys from the shots. Louie grabbed Phillip and threw the boy to the ground, and followed him down, landing on top of the big teen. Dexter leaped from his lawn chair and pulled Mike Woods to the ground with him. Joey had been standing, but knelt on one knee and began returning fire at the two-door Cadillac. Jessica grabbed Cynthia and pulled her down, while Charlie Li ran to protect Jackie. A small, round, red hole appeared in Charlie's shin as he dove to help Jessica. Both Megan and Misty produced weapons and returned fire, even as they both dove for cover. On the picnic table, the ketchup bottle exploded and splattered Megan thoroughly, while the dishes and food flew into the air from the bullets that struck them. The windows along the front of the house exploded into the home. Brandon and Patty, who had both been inside, slammed the door open and also began returning fire at the retreating trunk of the fleeing car.

And, just like that, it was over.

Joey called out, "Okay, who's hurt?"

"Shot in the leg," said Charlie. "Bullet passed through, but it stings like a motherf...It stings bad, I mean."

"Bullet nicked my arm, and nicked Phillip," said Louie. "Passed right through me, and hit him. We're both okay, though."

Dr. Bishop burst through the front door of the house.

"Anybody else?" asked Joey.

No one else answered him. They began picking themselves up from the ground and brushing themselves off. Sirens could be heard approaching in the distance.

Dr. Bishop looked around at the mess. He kept hearing a panting noise, like a dog or some other animal that had become winded. It finally dawned on him that it was coming from his right, on the porch with him. He turned to take a look.

Jennie Lou was sitting bolt upright in her wheelchair, taking short panting breaths. She was pale, and a tear was running down her face. Thinking that the girl was frightened, Dr. Bishop approached her. His eyes widened when he got closer to Jennie Lou.

"Joey!" he shouted. "Get *up* here! *Fast!*"

Joey looked, then raced to the porch. He was followed closely by Jackie, Louie, and Jessica. When he saw Jennie Lou, he almost cried out.

She was seated in her wheelchair. There was a bullet hole in her stomach, and it was bleeding...but not badly. In her chest was another bullet hole, and blood was pumping rhythmically, through it, in sync with her heartbeats, in large quantities. The seat of her wheelchair was already covered, and began spilling over onto the porch. Her panting was actually short breaths, as if she wasn't getting any oxygen.

"A bullet has punctured her aorta, the main artery leading from her heart," said Dr. Bishop. "She isn't getting any oxygen, because the blood is being pumped through the hole in her chest instead of through her body. Compression won't work, because she'd just bleed into her chest and abdominal cavity." He looked up at Joey, and Joey saw that the doctor had tears in his eyes. "I can't do anything for her, Joey...even if we were in a fully equipped operating theater. I wouldn't have enough time." He looked at Jackie, who had a look of shock on her face. "Miss Belew, if you want to say anything to her, now would be the time to do it. She has less than a minute."

Joey moved aside so that Jackie could be next to Jennie Lou. Jackie knelt and took Jennie's hand. Jennie, panting slowing, turned her head to Jackie.

"I love you, Jennie Lou," said Jackie. Tears were running freely down her face. "I love you. I wanted nothing but the best for you. I'm sorry this happened, sweet girl. I'd give anything if it was me instead. Please know that I love you."

Jennie Lou tried to smile through the deep breaths, but the best she could do was twitch the corners of her mouth.

Joey said quietly, "Jennie Lou, I promise you that Mickey Giambini will pay for this, if it's the last thing that I ever do."

The girl's breathing had slowed to a couple of breaths a minute. Her eyes had become glassy and distant. She took one last breath...and didn't take another.

Sixteen-year-old Jennie Lou Gwin died in the sunshine, on the front porch of her home, surrounded by people that loved her, on what had been a *good* day.

Chapter 14

At two forty-five the following afternoon, Rizzo came into Mickey Giambini's office. Giambini was staring out the big picture window at the city's skyline, daydreaming.

"Boss," said Rizzo.

Giambini looked at his assistant. "Whatcha got, Rizzo?"

"Boss, Leo Lesko is here...and he brought Vincent."

Giambini burst out laughing. "So, the lamb comes home after all! Oh, boy!" He laughed a bit more, straightened up, then looked at Rizzo. "Bring 'em, Rizzo...then stay with us."

Rizzo walked to the office door and opened it. He moved his head in a "come on" gesture, and Lesko and Vincent entered and stood beside the chairs in front of Giambini's desk. Rizzo moved to stand at the side of Giambini's desk. Giambini waved his hand, gesturing to the chairs, inviting the two men to sit down.

Lesko looked directly at Giambini. Giambini looked at Vincent. Vincent returned the look to Giambini.

"So," said Giambini. "Here we are."

The other men remained silent.

"I learned a long time ago," said Giambini, sounding remarkably educated and less thuggish, "that if you obsess about something, you open yourself up to defeat. Vincent, you and I were both guilty of that. I was obsessed with controlling something that I couldn't hold. I dunno *what* you were obsessed with, but it darn near ruined us both." He looked up at the men, shifting his gaze back and forth. "See, I *know* men like Justice. He's got iron in his spine, and he won't stop if he thinks he's right. But, a man like that...and like *me*...will keep his word, no matter what. He promised that if we released the Belew woman, it would stop. It did."

Vincent couldn't believe his ears. Giambini didn't know about the drive-by!

"All is forgiven," continued Giambini. He pointed at Vincent. "Just don't do nuthin' like this again, *capice?*"

Vincent nodded. "Yes, boss."

The office door slammed open, startling all four men.

Joey Justice stood there, arms extended, and a Glock in each hand. His eyes, visible under his furrowed brows, were angry. Behind him, carrying a pump shotgun, was Misty Wilhite.

"Hello, Giambini."

Giambini's mouth was wide open. *I got* people *outside there...why aren't they stopping him?*

"Joey Justice," said Giambini wonderingly. "But...you said it would be over if I turned her loose!"

Unseen by anyone inside the room, Misty nudged Joey in the back. She wanted to be sure that he had heard the remark...maybe this confrontation wouldn't turn into a bloodbath after all.

As if to dispel that thought, she heard a squeal of delight behind her, then two gunshots.

Joey smiled at Giambini. "Sounds like my partner, Megan, is getting a little excited. Somebody must have moved."

Lesko sat stock still, as if the situation was no concern of his. Rizzo was inching his hand toward his sport coat lapel.

Joey lifted a Glock and pointed it at Rizzo. "Mr. Rizzo, please don't. I would like to be able to deliver that bottle of Irish."

Rizzo raised his hands, then dropped them to his side.

Vincent felt a small tickle of dread at the base of his spine.

Joey took a couple of steps into the room, so that Misty could enter behind him and move to one side to help cover the men inside.

"Justice, what the *fuck* is this?" shouted Giambini. "What we did wasn't anything personal...it was just *business!* We took you at your word! We turned the Belew woman loose, and called it even! This shows your word ain't no damn good!"

Joey looked even angrier at the crime boss's words. He strode forcefully over to Giambini, took him by the arm, and spun him around to the big window behind his desk.

"See that building directly across from you?" asked Joey through clenched teeth.

"Yeah. So what?"

Joey took a small pair of binoculars from the equipment belt around his waist and handed it to Giambini. "Take a look. The open window, directly across from us."

Giambini looked at Joey, then looked through the binoculars as Joey had directed. When Giambini spotted the correct window, he saw Louie Washington, his arm in a sling, waving at him. Even worse, Marcus Moore, the company's FBI liason, was also waving. Behind them was lots of electronic eavesdropping equipment, and setups of cameras and telescopes. It was all aimed at Giambini's window. Giambini became furious inside. The FBI had found a way to watch him! Well, he'd settle that issue. Moses Stein owned that building. Giambini would send a couple of guys over and put Stein into the hospital.

As if reading Giambini's thoughts, Joey said, "Justice Security bought that building this morning from Moses Stein as an investment. We rented some office space to the FBI. I hope that's okay with you." He took back his binoculars. "As long as you do your 'business' from this building, you're going to have the FBI watching over you." Joey smiled at the furious crime boss. "It's just a matter of time now."

Giambini controlled himself with effort. "*Why,* Justice? I took you at your word!"

Joey lost his temper and began to shout. "And I took you at *yours,* you bastard! That little stunt yesterday proved that you can't leave things alone! You tried to kill Jackie, me, the kids, and my partners...and you say that I can't keep *my* word!" He pressed the barrel of one of his guns to the mob boss's temple. "I ought to kill you right now!"

Giambini knew that losing his temper right now would cost him his life. He struggled to keep his voice calm as he looked Joey in the eyes. "I give you my word of honor, *on record,* that I have not tried to kill you. I have not tried to harm you or the Belew woman in any way since you left with her last Saturday night."

Joey saw the truth in the older man's eyes. "Maybe it wasn't you, and maybe it wasn't *ordered* by you. But it was someone in your organization. You didn't keep a tight enough rein on your people! Somebody took it upon themselves to try to wipe us out, maybe to try to impress you...but I hold *you* responsible!" Joey took a couple of steps back from Giambini, and gestured to the office window. "So, Justice Security bought that building. And we rented office space to the FBI. We'll let *them* take *you* down." He stepped forward and lowered his voice. "I want the ones involved in the drive-by. I'll take care of them."

Giambini was fighting his temper, and almost lost the battle. "Justice, I understand your frustration...*but I can't help you!*"

A low chuckle came from one of the chairs in front of Giambini's desk. Everyone's attention turned to Vincent.

"*I* did the drive-by, Justice," said Vincent quietly. "*I* did it! And I'd do it again! That fuckin' Belew woman has been nuthin' but trouble from me from day *one! And I hope I fuckin' killed the bitch!*"

"*Vincent!*" shouted Giambini, who finally had someone that could take his pent-up anger. "I told you to leave that woman strictly alone! *Now look at the trouble you've caused, you fuckin' idiot!*"

"Vincent," said Lesko. "I'm very disappointed in you."

"Wanna know why I did it?" asked Vincent. "Wanna know the answer? *Boss?* Because you ain't fit no more to run this organization! I can run it better than you by a long shot! You was holdin' me back with that fuckin' Belew bitch! We could had all gold that goose could give, but *you* wouldn't let me rough her up! Then, when *this* fuckwad," he pointed a thumb at Joey, "showed up, you got all scared, and let the golden goose go! Well, if *we* ain't gonna use her, *nobody's* gonna use her!"

Giambini's face turned red from anger. He began spluttering, but before he could say anything understandable, Joey began walking around the desk and behind the two occupied chairs, coming around to Vincent's right side. Vincent was observing Joey through angry and defiant eyes.

"Yeah? Whatcha gonna do, Mr. Rent-A-Cop?" said Vincent. "Can't kill me, 'cause the 'boss' here would kill you...*and* the FBI would put you away for a few years to boot!"

Joey met Vincent's eyes with his own. Vincent cringed slightly at the fire he saw in them.

"You didn't kill Jackie," said Joey. "You never even came close. You *did* wound Louie...a man that works for me named Charlie Li...and a seventeen-year-old boy who has beaten you before. Nothing to worry about. Except for one little thing...you *also* killed a harmless, sixteen-year-old girl that had *just* discovered a bright future ahead of her." Joey put his Glock against the bridge of Vincent's nose. "She was my foster daughter." Joey cocked his weapon. "This is nothing business...just personal." He pulled the trigger.

The entry point of the bullet made a small hole in the bridge of Vincent's nose. The gasses that came from the firing of the weapon caused Vincent's head and eyes to bulge slightly, and, as the bullet mushroomed on its path through Vincent's brain, its passage caused an exit wound two and a half times as large as the entry wound. A large piece of Vincent's brain exited his head at the same time as the spent bullet, along with a couple of chunks of his skull. Vincent, who was now far beyond the point of observing anything again, slumped into his seat, with his head hanging over the back of the chair. The silence of the office was broken only by the dripping of Vincent's blood.

Joey lowered his weapon and looked at Misty. She nodded at him. It was time to go.

Joey turned to Giambini. The crime boss was standing with his mouth open, as if he couldn't believe that Joey had killed Vincent...even though Giambini had planned to kill the man himself.

"Giambini," said Joey.

Giambini turned his attention to Joey.

"We're leaving now. I'm satisfied."

Joey and Misty backed out of the door.

Rizzo, Lesko, and Giambini were silent for several moments. Then, Giambini turned to the two men.

"I want you two to get the word out right now," he said quietly. "I don't care *what* Fernandez is offering. I will pay five million dollars to whoever brings me Joey Justice's head on a platter." He gestured to Vincent's body. "And get somebody to take *that* to the sausage factory and get it processed with the other hogs."

Chapter 15

As the casket was lowered into the grave, Joey looked around the cemetery. Brown Justice Security uniforms could be seen surrounding the entire property. Joey hated that it had to be done, but he didn't want anything interrupting Jennie Lou's final farewell.

A couple of hours after they had left Giambini's building, Joey had met up with Marcus Moore.

"You just keep racking up the money, Joey," said Marcus.

Joey looked puzzled. "What do you mean?"

Marcus chuckled. "Word is that Giambini has offered five million dollars for whoever can kill you. Add the Fernandez money to that, and you're worth fifteen million bucks dead." He shook his head. "Realistically, buddy, you're gonna have *lots* of people looking to kill you. I truthfully would not want to be in your shoes right now."

Joey had pondered that for a while. People trying to kill him was nothing new, but the money offered by those two major players had upped the ante quite a bit. He actually had to take that into account whenever he went anywhere in the city.

The funeral today was a somber affair. Jackie Belew and Mike Woods sat next to Joey, and Misty sat on Joey's other side. Cynthia, Tommy, and Nicky also sat, but Phillip chose to stand next to Louie. Phillip was rocking slowly back and forth, gaining speed and keening a bit as his foster sister was placed slowly into her final resting place. Dexter, Megan, and Jessica stood beside Turk, Charlie Li, and Marcus Moore. Brandon King and Patty Ferguson stood behind them. Dr. Bishop stood off to one side, beside Dr. Caleb Mitchell. Many were crying.

Services had been graveside, and non-denominational. The officiating minister, a Methodist elder of Jackie's acquaintance, delivered a few platitudes that were meant to comfort the family, but didn't. Each child had been given time to say a few words about their foster sister, and each had related a story that described Jennie Lou's kindness to each of them. Phillip had been able to blurt out that he had loved his sister, but that was all.

It was enough.

It was Thursday...two days after Justice Security's invasion of Giambini's empire. No one had seen or heard anything about Vincent. No body had been discovered, and no body had washed up on the bay's shores. None of the FBI people watching the place had reported anything leaving the building large enough to be Vincent's body.

Joey had made no secret of the fact that he had killed Vincent. When he had confessed the killing to Marcus, Marcus had been blunt.

"He's a mob guy, Joey. A killer, a thief, and a racketeer. No great loss to society at large, in other words. If...and I want to emphasize *if*...a body turns up, the death will be investigated, and it will be ruled a mob killing. We'll pull in the usual suspects, and we'll question them. Nobody will know anything, and it will remain unsolved. Don't worry about it."

The man officiating the funeral was wrapping up his remarks with the usual "ashes to ashes" line from the Bible, just as Jennie Lou's casket stopped its downward descent. Each foster sibling held a single yellow rose, and Jackie, Mike, and Joey each held a red rose. The funeral director asked the children and the three adults to stand, and to pass beside the open grave. As they did, each of them dropped their rose onto the casket as a final goodbye. Joey wore sunglasses, but Misty noticed a single tear rolling down Joey's cheek.

There weren't any school friends in attendance. Jennie didn't make lasting friends at school, so none came to mourn. Her foster siblings were the only children at the funeral.

Jackie stopped. She had wiped her tears, and wanted to say a few things. Mike supported her with his strong arms. The children continued walking through the cemetery, making their way to the other side of a rather large monument. Joey glanced at them as they walked.

"I just wanted to say another thank you for all you people have done," said Jackie.

Joey actually tuned Jackie out. He was concentrating.

Something about the kids was wrong.

Cynthia, Tommy, Nicky, and Phillip, all walking behind that monument.

Nothing really surprising in that. The four of them had become very close in the wake of Jennie Lou's death.

The four of them.

Joey's eyes widened as he realized what was bothering him.

"Will you folks please excuse me for a moment?" asked Joey. "I'd like to speak to the children. It's important."

Misty looked at Joey, a question in her eyes. Joey shook his head, indicating that there was no problem. Misty relaxed. Jackie and Mike both assured him that they were fine with it.

Joey walked in the same direction that the children had gone.

All five of them.

A little brown-haired girl, about ten, had been leading the four siblings.

When Joey rounded the corner, all he saw were the four. The little brown-haired girl was not there.

"She's gone, Joey," said Nicky.

"Her name is Madeline," said Tommy.

Cynthia said, "She's an angel."

"An angel," said Joey flatly.

"She said you'd notice her, and would come to ask us about her," said Tommy.

"Yeah," said Nicky. "She said she just wanted to let us know that we don't need to cry for Jennie Lou. She said that Jennie Lou misses us, but is with her parents again, and is really happy in heaven."

"And Madeline said that you'd meet her soon enough. What does that mean, Joey?" asked Cynthia.

Joey smiled. "I don't know, Cynthia." He knelt in front of her. "Do you really believe that little girl was an angel?"

Cynthia nodded vigorously. "Oh, yes. She said you wouldn't believe what she was, so she gave Phillip a little present to convince you."

Joey stood and went to the big boy. "What was your present, Phillip?"

Phillip, who had been looking down during Joey's conversations with his siblings, looked up and into Joey's eyes. There was a *presence* there, a sense that Phillip was really *here,* looking out from those bright eyes.

"She gave me the gift of clarity, Joey," said Phillip with no trouble at all. His voice was deep and melodic. "She has given me a couple of minutes of clarity, so that I can communicate with you on an equal level." He shook his head. "Wow. I have so much to say, I don't know where to start!" He turned to his siblings. "Since I only have a couple of minutes, I want to tell you all that I love you. I love every one of you with all my heart. And you can tell Jackie that I love her, too, and that I'll be glad when she marries Mike Woods." He turned to Joey. "Joey Justice, I want to thank you and your people for never treating me as if I'm retarded. People have problems seeing the difference between *autistic* and *retarded*. Retarded is not a word I would use for special needs children, but I'm speaking for brevity, since I only have a couple of minutes." He spread his hands. "*All* of you have always made me feel like I'm part of the family, a part of *something,* and that I'm not a piece of furniture." A tear came to his eye. "Jennie Lou understood me from the start, and made me feel special...awww, *crap!*" He wiped his eyes. "I feel the trap circling again...the clarity is wearing off. I love you all! I..." His eyes lost their brightness and began turning inward again. He began rocking back and forth again, as he looked at nothing in particular.

Joey stood staring at Phillip, mouth open in wonder. At that moment, he believed. He believed in angels, miracles, and God in his heaven. He closed his mouth. He looked at the other children.

"Wow," he said. "Let's get you guys out of here, okay?"

As the children started back, Misty met them halfway. She noticed Joey's face and said, "What is it?"

Joey shook his head. "Later, honey, okay?"

Misty looked puzzled, but nodded. "Okay."

Joey's cell phone rang as they caught up with Jackie Blue.

"This is Joey."

"Joey, this is Tony. Boss, when are you coming back to the building?"

"We should be there in about thirty minutes or so. Why?"

"Just hurry. You are *not* going to believe this!"

ABOUT THE AUTHOR: T. M. Bilderback is a former radio announcer with a number of story ideas running around inside his head, most based on, or inspired by, classic songs. The author currently resides in Tennessee, and is writing feverishly in order to banish these stories from his head and into book form, before they drive him screaming into the street.

Other works by T. M. Bilderback

N<u>*icholas Turner*</u>
  If You Could Read My Mind
<u>**Justice Security**</u>
Mama Told Me Not To Come
Someone Saved My Life Tonight
Jackie Blue
Wake Me Up Before You Go-Go
Saturday In The Park
MacArthur Park
The Little Drummer Boy
The Night Chicago Died
Jim Dandy
Cow Patty
Hell's Bells
Black Dog
Lido Shuffle
<u>**Tales Of Sardis County**</u>
Don't Come Around Here No More
Junior's Farm
The Devil's In The Details
I'm Your Boogie Man
<u>**Colonel Abernathy's Tales**</u>
The Lion Sleeps Tonight
Heart Of Glass
<u>**Other Stories**</u>
The Wreck Of The Edmund Fitzgerald
Gold
Hot Child In The City
Eli's Coming
<u>**Other Novels**</u>
Empty Eyes
<u>**Story Collections**</u>
Greatest Hits